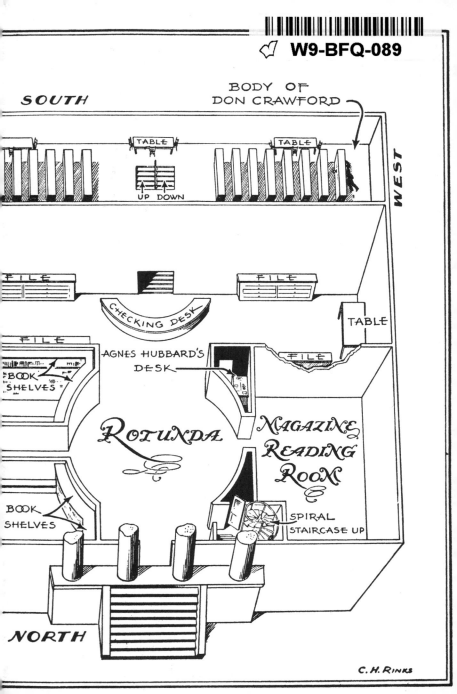

SOUTH

BODY OF
DON CRAWFORD

WEST

TABLE

TABLE

UP DOWN

FILE

FILE

CHECKING DESK

TABLE

AGNES HUBBARD'S
DESK

FILE

BOOK
SHELVES

ROTUNDA

MAGAZINE
READING
ROOM

BOOK
SHELVES

SPIRAL
STAIRCASE UP

NORTH

C. H. RINKS

MURDER IN THE STACKS

MURDER IN
THE STACKS

by

MARION BOYD HAVIGHURST

Miami University
Oxford, Ohio 45056
1989

Preface

The reprinting of *Murder in the Stacks* has been made possible through gifts to the Miami University fund in celebration of the memory of Marion Boyd Havighurst, who dedicated her book in 1934, "To Walter, who scorns detective stories, I offer this one, without a detective."

Fifty-five years later, this facsimile printing is also dedicated to Walter Havighurst, teacher, writer, mentor, inspiration for generations of students who were in his classes or who came under his influence on campus, and beloved friend of faculty and townspeople in "a particularly charming spot" of middle America.

Beyond funding, a great number of friends of Walter have supported this project. These friends have felt the charming and delightful murder mystery, written on the Miami University campus, using the town of Oxford as the model for its setting and the campus library as the scene of the crime, should be available for alumni who remember the campus as it was, and for today's students who have the imagination to think of the campus as it has been.

We cannot name everyone, but those who have been mainstays in this venture must be recognized: L. Scott and Margaret Teets Bailey (MU '48, '47), Edward M. and Anne Amos Brown (MU '31, '32). We appreciate the support and assistance of Curator of the Walter Havighurst Special Collections Helen C. Ball, Dean and University Librarian Judith A.

Sessions, Director of Audio Visual Services William L. King, Assistant to the Curator Frances D. McClure for seeing this book through publication, and especially that of Walter Havighurst, who has given all rights to this book to the University.

Paul G. Pearson, President
Miami University
February, 1989

When we first married, Marion and I talked about what we wanted to do in a five-year period; it was good for both of us. As it turned out, we both came to a book-size publication within just five years after we began to share our aspirations.

Murder in the Stacks, "a detective story without a detective," was the first novel published by Marion, whose collected poems *Silver Wands*, was published in the Yale Series of Younger Poets. One reviewer had written: "Each poem expresses something of Miss Boyd's own personality, together with her intimate appreciation of nature." She had already decided her future writing should be more of observation than introspection. *Murder* was the result.

I was working on *Pier 17* when she got interested in an experience that had happened to Ned (E.W. King, Miami University Librarian) who collected children's books.* We had spent an afternoon with Ned and Faith King who lived just two houses from us at the time. Although they were never likely to talk about their bookish interest and searches, they began to tell us this story. He had acquired from a New York bookdealer a copy of Charles Lamb's *The King and Queen of Hearts*, published in 1805. A small, thin, paperbound volume, it got buried in the papers on Mr. King's desk in the old Alumni Library. One day a London book catalog arrived in the mail that showed the 1805 title listed at £1,500—a small fortune in the 1930s. Ned King and his wife began to search for their copy, but they never found it. It could have been slipped into a larger book and lost

*This collection is now the E.W. and Faith King Collection of Juvenile Literature in the University Library.

to sight, or slipped into a bookstore catalog that was then discarded.

That evening, Marion, who liked mystery stories talked about writing a mystery based on the disappearance of a valuable little chapbook—*The King and Queen of Hearts*. So, while the Kings searched for their book, she began writing *Murder in the Stacks*, a mystery of theft and violence on a campus that resembled Miami University.

Alumni who were students in the 1930s will surely recognize the description of the campus, some of the characters such as the nightwatchman, and even President Upham's Scotty dog that wore the Phi Beta Kappa key on his collar.

For many years, even though the book has been noted in occasional library publications, the only copies that were available for the public were housed in the non-circulating collections of the University Libraries. It is heartening to know that students on campus today will be able to have a copy of the book. It is written in the style of the '30s, without profanity and sex, but with a gentility that even serious readers of murder mysteries will enjoy.

Walter Havighurst
Shadowy Hills. Oxford, Ohio
February 6, 1989

There is a faint movement through an open space —
And lovely white ghosts wake mysteriously
Like white thought smiling through gray memory.

White Dusk by Marion M. Boyd, 1923

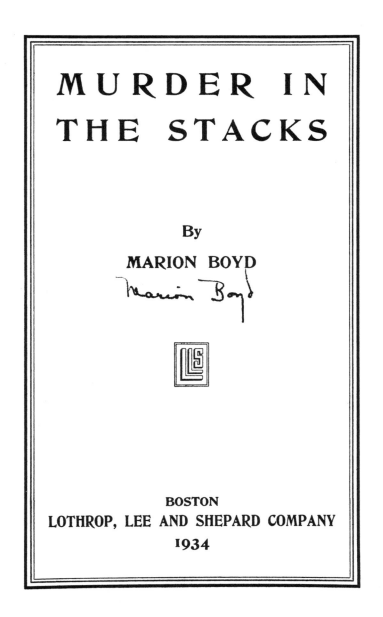

MURDER IN THE STACKS

By

MARION BOYD

Marion Boyd

BOSTON
LOTHROP, LEE AND SHEPARD COMPANY
1934

TO WALTER,

who scorns detective stories,
I offer this one, without a detective

CHAPTER I

IN a particularly charming spot in one of our much maligned middle western states, the little college town of Kingsley snuggles warmly down among its wooded hills. Streams meander slowly about the countryside, and several unexpected lakes dot the valleys. Beech trees fling a golden mist of buds over the village in spring, and in fall their russet harvest carpets the streets and campus. The town itself is like a bit of New England strangely transplanted westward a few hundred miles. It has its village green, its dignified white church, its rows of shops strung like the backdrop of a stage setting along one street, its old white houses with beautiful fan doorways, its campus strewn with ancient red brick buildings. And over it all there broods a calm serenity, challenged though it is by the thousands of students who pour through it year after year.

To live there, I had learned, was to eat of the fruit of the lotus. Like myself many had come expecting to remain but a year or two, but year after year, drifting by in a kind of quiet enchantment, found them still lingering. Many had grown old there, giving only an occasional and involuntary sigh for the worlds they had failed to conquer. Unsuspicious of the languor about to overtake me, I had charged forth, a shining new Ph.D. trailing after my name, to teach English at Kingsley University. Five years had passed and I still remained. And young though I was, I found myself sinking into a contented lethargy more fitting to persons of middle age. I had friends of whom I was fond, work that was congenial to me, surroundings which pleased me. I led a complacent bachelor existence, but I felt none of the poignancy of life, none of its tragedy, none of its ecstasy.

Thus situated I remained until the spring of 1934 when with complete unexpectedness my complacency was disrupted. It was not that I was less charmed with my surroundings. On the contrary I was more than ever aware of the loveliness of nature and humanity—at least of one specimen of humanity. But the shock confused, I might even say unbalanced, me a bit.

For example, I recall that all I felt that beautiful morning of June the eighth was a perfectly banal desire to wander around the university campus and chant with the poet, "What is so rare as a day in June — " and all the rest of it. I had wakened early (six-thirty is early for me) and the rapture I felt at a sunny morning, at the sound of birds singing, was entirely unacademic. My rapture was also, as I learned all too soon, utterly out of keeping with the gruesome discovery I was to make before the day was three hours gone. But when I first opened my eyes I was filled with the sort of emotion I had occasionally envied in some of my students. There was, however, nothing vicarious in my enjoyment that morning. I woke to a complete sense of elation.

Further sleep was impossible. I lay for a moment listening to the song of a cardinal outside my window, and I repeated to myself the sentence that Carla Robinson had spoken yesterday. I had been standing at the door of her office on the second floor of the library when she had softly enunciated the words.

"I'm going to teach the first six weeks of summer school," she had said, and my heart stirred as much to see the color flood suddenly into her cheeks as at the information her words conveyed.

I remembered it all deliciously that morning as I leaped out of bed and began throwing on my clothes. I dressed hurriedly but quietly, for I did not want to disturb old Dr. Tyndale, who was head of the History department and who occupied a room next to mine, or Miss MacIntyre, the owner of the tree-shaded colonial house where we lived. As I let myself silently out of the house, I saw coming up the walk Dr. Tyndale's little Scotty, "Napoleon." At the street gate stood his ubiquitous companion, an enormously tall, thin canine with a long curving tail. He was owned by the night watchman of the university, and he seemed to have no counterpart in dogdom, being apparently part wolf hound, part great Dane, a frightening creature of dark gray color whose thin uncanny face wore an expression of terrifying and almost human anxiety. There was something obscurely unnatural in the companionship of these dogs. At my appearance the enormous hound took his departure, while the little Scotty squatted on the doorstep looking after him.

There was such ineluctable dignity in his pose that I gazed down at him for a moment with amazement. He was completely indifferent to my presence, watching complacently the departure of his long-legged friend. A beam of sunlight glancing through the leaves onto Napoleon shot a blinding ray into my eyes. Stooping to pat him I saw something gold attached to his collar. A Phi Beta Kappa key! "By Jove, even the dogs of this town flaunt them," I laughed to myself. Some student prank I thought as I read the name "Oscar Bartlett" engraved on the tiny emblem. One never knew what to expect next in a college community. Well, Oscar Bartlett would be hunting a lost key some of these days, and his mischievous friends would never reveal their part in the prank.

"I trust you value the honor," I said gravely to the little dog. "It is one never conferred upon your namesake." He favored me with a brief glance as I made off up College Avenue toward George and Harry's Coffee Shop, whistling like any carefree college boy.

Harry himself greeted me. "Glad college is out, Mr. Allen?" he inquired, himself a little lugubrious now that the season of easy dimes was drawing to a close. And as he slapped the eggs in front of me, he sighed rather enviously. "I suppose you'll be going on a trip soon," he ventured.

"No, no trip for me till August," I answered gaily. "I'm teaching in summer school the first term."

Harry looked duly sympathetic. Twenty-four hours earlier I would have pulled a face long enough to bring tears to any waiter's eyes. But now all I could muster was the remark, "Well, a job's not to be sniffed at these days."

"That's right, sir," he began and was, no doubt, ready to launch himself into a dissertation on the troubles of the entire Greek race, but the screen door slammed and the good old class of '28 came streaming in all dressed like bandits and ready to make whoopee with the coffee and doughnuts.

"Good Lord," I thought, "Alumni Day!" But even that appalling remembrance, which had temporarily slipped my mind, was not enough to put me in a bad humor. As everyone who lives in a college community knows, there is no time so hated by its inhabitants as Commencement with its attendant hordes of alumni running around like squirrels digging up long-buried nuts.

But that morning their exuberance could not daunt me. To be sure I had been graduated from my own college only a few years, and in that length of time even the veins of an English professor have not become utterly desiccated.

I winked at George as I slammed down my thirty cents and looked enviously at the swashbuckling costumes of dear old '28. Had I been garbed as they I could have capered down the street and across the campus with any antics that suggested themselves, but in my everyday linen suit it was necessary to preserve as dignified a course as possible.

The task ahead of me was none too inviting. A term paper on "The Influence of the Graveyard Poets on Bryant", handed in the day before, bore every mark of plagiarism, and while the words were familiar I could not quite place them. That meant hours in the stacks of the library hunting up possible references before I could present actual proof of dishonesty. Kingsley University was insistent upon integrity of scholarship. Such a paper as had been handed to me must be tracked to its original source. I had no desire to tackle the job; yet I wanted it finished as soon as possible, for I entertained the fondest hopes of having Alumni Day Collation with Carla Robinson. As a matter of fact — but all that can come later in its proper chronology of that sunny day which for me at least turned into such a black nightmare.

Just then, however, as I swung along the slant walk, my thoughts were all with Carla. I had known her only since February when she had come to fill a vacancy left in the French department by the illness of a Miss Henderson, a lady of quite a different aspect. From the beginning — I may as well confess it — I had been amazingly aware of the existence of Carla Robinson. I had, I believe, the reputation at Kingsley of being impervious to the charms of co-eds, charms which, I may say in passing, bloomed with the profusion of the dandelion. That excess was, perhaps, a deterrent to me. But among the three hundred members of the faculty, of which seventy-five were women, there was not this wealth of pulchritude. So that at the first faculty tea of the second semester Carla Robinson was as noticeable as a crocus in a somewhat weedy lawn. Many were cognizant of the fact. As for me, I was, as the students say, knocked for a loop. And in that uncomfortable state I had remained, realizing that in June I would flatten to earth with the return of Miss Henderson to take up her summer duties. But by some miraculous stroke of fortune Miss Henderson remained ill. Only yesterday Carla had been asked to stay on. I liked to recall how swiftly she had imparted the news to me.

Thinking these thoughts, and being already five years gone in academic absent-mindedness, I now found myself shaking the door knob at the front entrance of the library. But of course the door was locked. It is not supposed to open until nine o'clock, when the janitor, one Abraham Hunt, inserts the colossal key. It was now barely eight. I should have known before attempting an honest entrance that the somewhat unethical manner I gain access to the library at off hours was the only means suitable for this occasion. Fortunately no one was about to see my ignominious retreat down the granite steps, and I had soon circled the building to the spot where the shrubbery grows thick before the rear windows of the basement row of stacks. In this gloomy region there are at least three windows which to my knowledge have not been locked for five years, and while not responsible for this bit of carelessness, I had frequently taken advantage of it. In view of the frightful discovery that was later made I solemnly rebuked myself for my failure to report these unlocked windows then or at any subsequent time. But on that Friday morning it seemed only a convenient and very private entry.

The windows all slid up with great ease and quietness, though never before that day had I found one of them open. It was but a step over the sill, and I slid myself over quickly and made my way to the next higher level of the stacks and to the east end where I knew from former usage that the reference books on the Graveyard poets were to be found.

Above me were three more levels of stacks, and on each floor the shelves rose to a height of about six feet. There were on each level about twenty rows of shelves divided by aisles four or five feet wide. These transverse aisles opened at either end on longer ones that ran the entire length of that portion of the library. The long inner aisle was bounded by an inside wall of the building. The outer aisle was lit by windows, but the light that found its way through the dusty panes was dim, giving to the interior a kind of faint twilight singularly appropriate to these bound thoughts of writers many of whom were long since dead.

Hunting up the books necessary to my task, I made a pile of them on one of the tables placed between the windows of the outer wall. Then I began my search for the source of the paper in question. This proved to be more onerous than I had anticipated, for with diabolical cunning my pupil had knitted together verbatim paragraphs from several authorities.

I had been at work an hour, as I now know, when I was conscious of heels tap-tapping on the opaque glass of the floor. The pleasurable notion that they might belong to Carla made me turn my head. I had just time to catch a glimpse of the slim back of the desk clerk, Agnes Hubbard, before she turned to go between two shelves of books at the west end. For a moment or two there was silence. I know now that she was seeking the number of a certain book. Then there was a faint cry, the sound of a heavy book falling, and a duller·scraping thud as of a body slipping to the floor.

I ran the length of the aisle and found the form of Agnes Hubbard stretched in a dead faint on the floor. A thick book lay at her side, and as I stooped to lift the girl, my eyes went automatically to the space left by the removal of the volume. I saw the cause of her unconsciousness, and for an instant my own senses reeled.

There hanging limp and loose from the sleeve of a tan suit was a man's hand. It dangled in a manner frightfully suggestive. Instinctively I reached out to touch it. It was as cold as the steel shelf over which it hung.

CHAPTER II

ALTHOUGH I have never confessed it to Agnes Hubbard, I think that the bump on her head from which she suffered for the next three or four days was due not to her original faint but to the force with which I then dropped her head.

A hand was hanging limply from a sleeve. I thought I recognized that hand with its gold seal ring. And a nameless horror gripped me. Was it attached to a body? It looked disembodied there, but the thought that it had been amputated was too sinister to dwell upon. The rows of books completely hid from view anything concealed behind them. Did the arm dangle merely from space, or was there a body on the floor behind those books?

I suppose I did not actually tick off these questions one at a time as I now write them. But later, recalling my sensations, I was conscious that each one of them had entered into the decision that caused my next action. For I left Agnes Hubbard as she was, lying on the cold glass floor with the heavy book at her side, and urged by some involuntary primitive instinct I tiptoed around the shelf of books.

It was no vacancy of space that greeted my gaze. The figure was stretched full length on its right side, the right arm flung out, the left plunged through a row of books, as if, slipping and sliding as he fell, Donald Crawford had sought to catch himself before his head struck the heavy steel shelf, slightly displaced near the floor, against which his head now rested.

I stood gazing at him, my mind a turmoil of confusion and of fright. Donald Crawford, assistant librarian, a gentle blonde recluse, but strangely enough my friend. The one friend, he had once told me, to whom he had ever confided anything, and precious little that anything had been.

I knew that he was dead. The touch of that cold hand had told me that certainly. But in what manner dead? How could Don, that constant walker on glass floors, have slipped on this one and at the exact spot where a protruding shelf met his head? Perhaps it was because of something he had confided to me on the preceding day that an instant fear rose in my mind. I know that I looked carefully at the floor to see if it bore marks of a slipping, slithering misstep. There was no such mark. I even took a few steps myself and purposely slid. Later I came to regret the impulse. For the marks that I made on the floor were naturally misinterpreted. As I looked down at the heavy glass, the results of my slipping were plainly visible. They showed as plainly as tracks on an icy pavement.

And then, with no further consideration of the re-

sults of my action, I bent over the form of my friend.
I knew that I must not disturb the figure. Some subconscious remembrance of detective stories I had read
warned me of that. But the lifeless form of Donald
Crawford seemed to speak to me, to me alone, to
solve this mystery, if mystery it were. The words he
had spoken to me the day before as we walked across
the campus together at noon rang in my ears.

"Tom" he had said, and I have never seen his eyes
so full of light, "I believe I've got hold of something
valuable. Quite by accident I've got possession of a
thing that might make me independent for several
years. It would give me leisure to write my book."

And when I had pressed him for further details he
had only smiled. How well I recalled that slow smile
and the shake of his head.

"No," he had answered. "No more now. I want to
be perfectly sure. And besides there's a rather nice
ethical point involved. I have to think it out first."

And here he lay dead at my feet. Not much ethics
in that, I fancied.

There was something about that still, crumpled figure that called mutely to me. And there was a piece
of paper protruding from the pocket of his coat that
made me stoop, and with small regard for consequences made me pull it from his pocket. It was a
plain manila envelope. There was no writing on it,
but even as I stuffed it in my own pocket I noticed
something about it that seemed unusual, unlike my
friend. He was peculiarly methodical in opening
letters. Often enough in the three years of our ac-

quaintance I had watched him. Invariably he would tear a narrow strip from one end of the envelope and carefully extract the contents. Then after reading it, he would as carefully insert it in the envelope. Up to this point one would have judged him to be neat to a fault. But then he would do a queer thing. He would cram the envelope into any pocket where there was room. For days he would go about, his pockets stuffed with communications, bills and advertisements. Eventually he would decide to wear another suit. Then the contents of the one he had been wearing would be destroyed, and he would begin a fresh collection. The pigeonholes of his desk were almost free of correspondence. He used his clothes as a filing cabinet. It was a trait which had never failed to amuse and interest me. Now it assumed a new significance. I could see that the two pockets of his coat were crammed with envelopes, which I had no doubt were neatly torn at one end. But this envelope was different. It had been torn open hastily so that a jagged tear ran down half the face of the envelope.

My entire inspection of the body had occupied far less time than it takes to tell about it — only a minute or two at the most. As I rounded the high shelf to the section where Agnes Hubbard lay, not a shadow of regret tinged my mind at the guilty knowledge that I had just taken from the pocket of my dead friend an envelope to the possession of which I had not the slightest right. My only feeling was one of eagerness to get to my room and see what the envelope contained.

As I lifted the slight form of the girl, my eye caught a minute glitter on the glass floor. Resting the girl on one knee, I stooped and reached toward it. Two tiny gold links lay in my hand. I dropped them carefully into the envelope in my pocket.

There was no one in the stacks as I carried the limp form of the girl up to the next level and toward the swinging doors that opened onto the checking desk and the lobby of the library. Nor was there any one at the desk. But to the right I saw Miss Chase, one of the assistant librarians, jotting down numbers from one of the drawers of the card catalogue. She looked up, and I saw her face go pale as she saw my flaccid burden.

"Bring her in here," she said, and held open the door to the general office. "What's happened to her, Mr. Allen?"

"She's fainted, that's all," I said, trying to keep out of my voice the horror of that grim cause of her collapse. There were several girls in the librarian's office, all waiting their orders for the day. The final check-up of books at the end of a school year is no inconsiderable amount of work. With its five or six desks, counters, tables and innumerable shelves, the place seemed crowded.

"She'll come to in a minute, I think," I said as one of the girls ran for water and two others bent to work over the slight form of Agnes Hubbard where I had laid her on a table.

Mr. Denman, the head librarian, was at his desk. He hurried over toward the group, and I noticed how his dark eyes flickered from one girl to another. Quite a Lothario, our Mr. Denman, with his dark foreign-looking face, his clipped mustache and his immaculate clothing. He much preferred girls to boys as his student assistants. I drew him aside.

"Come with me a minute," I said, and led him off toward the stacks. "Something rather awful has happened. Donald Crawford is crumpled up on the floor back there." In a few steps I had guided him to that ghastly corner.

He took one look at that figure. "My God, man, he's hurt," he cried, and before I could stop him, he had turned Don's body over on his back. The limp hand slithered out of the shelf to rest on the floor.

"Not hurt — dead," I answered. But he knew that for himself now. His hand had rested for an instant on that still, cold face. He raised awe-stricken eyes to mine.

Behind me I heard a little gasp. I had thought we were alone, but Miss Chase had followed us. I should have foreseen that she would. If there is ever a place where that little snub nose does not poke, or where those blue, wide-open eyes do not look, I have yet to discover it. She had seemed perpetually omnipresent whenever in the past months I had ascended the curving stairs to Carla Robinson's office. And now here she was again where she had no business to be. I had taken it for granted that she would remain with Agnes Hubbard. Of course she had not.

At her gasp of astonishment I turned. It would have been natural for those blue eyes to be wide with horror—which they were. But I thought at the time that I saw in them more than horror. A panic-stricken look of terror lay behind the natural emotion.

"Oh, you shouldn't have moved him!" She almost cried the words. Mark Denman, still on his knees beside Don, raised his dark eyes and looked at her coldly.

"I did not realize that he was dead, Miss Chase," he said sternly.

Bertha Chase had not moved. She stood in her first attitude of amazement. The fingers of one hand moved nervously over her face. "Of course — of course not," she agreed, her voice shaking, "but — "

I was to remember later that one word, "but", and to wonder what clause of enlightenment it was about to introduce. At that instant, however, we were interrupted. Footsteps came along the rear aisle of the stacks, and suddenly there appeared around the corner of the shelves two persons looking as if they had just stepped out of a novel of the nineties. And though I was familiar with the appearance of both of these elderly persons, they seemed at that moment to be more apparitions than realities. Miss MacIntyre looked much as usual, dressed in a starched linen skirt that flared at the bottom, a shirt waist with leg-of-mutton sleeves and a stiffly boned high collar, the whole topped by an out-of-date, flower-laden hat. But in that dim, book-lined aisle, charged with the tragedy of our discovery, the oddity of her appearance struck me with sudden force. Dr. Tyndale's large form loomed beside her. He was a trifle stooped, his linen suit crumpled and baggy, his worn brown shoes shuffling over the glass floor. Only his high, stiff collar and bow tie added an immaculate note that matched the fastidious neatness of the woman beside him. They made an incongruous picture standing there, so incongruous indeed that I was impressed less by their presence at that particular moment than by the fact that never before then had I regarded my two house mates with the impartial regard of a mere observer.

They stood looking at us and at that still form on the cold floor, and on their faces I saw that same look that must have frozen my own features when I first came upon the body of Donald Crawford. Miss MacIntyre's sweet, faded face with its high patrician nose was paler even than usual, though she was the first to gain her voice.

"What is it? What does it mean? Is some one dead?" Her brown, bird-like eyes darted from one to the other of us.

Mark Denman answered her, rather shortly, I thought. "It's Mr. Crawford," he said. "Yes, he's dead."

"You mean your young assistant?" Dr. Tyndale bent forward and peered at the floor. He blinked his near-sighted eyes and wiped off his glasses. "How did it happen?"

"We don't know. He must have slipped and fallen. His head evidently struck here on this steel shelf. There's no knowing how long he's been dead."

A kind of low moan came from Miss Chase.

"A terrible thing, a terrible thing." Dr. Tyndale began to repeat himself in mumbling tones as was his habit.

His muttering was interrupted by Miss MacIntyre. "Yes, that's exactly what happened. Oh, the poor young man! You can see here where he slipped."

I saw her pointing to the scraped place on the floor where I had tried my sliding experiment. Too late I regretted that impulsive action. An explanation now was out of the question. What would they think if I should confess that I had made that mark, sliding around experimentally on the glass floor near the body of my dead friend?

I caught Dr. Tyndale's eyes peering at me in a questioning manner, and suddenly I felt very hot in the face.

"Shouldn't the president be notified?" Miss Chase's round blue eyes assumed an important expression as she asked the question.

"Certainly, Miss Chase. I was just going to speak of it." Mark Denman was still curt in his remarks. "But it's a bit hard to know how best to reach him. He's reviewing the Alumni procession just now, you'll remember."

"Perhaps — " I began. But Mr. Denman cut me off.

"It's up to you, Professor Tyndale," he announced. "By seniority and position it's best that you inform President Mittoff."

I saw an expression of outrage flicker across Dr. Tyndale's face. He was insistent always on his correct title, and he felt it a personal insult to be called "Professor." Mr. Denman always delighted in overlooking this small pretension.

To Dr. Tyndale's stuttered remonstrance he paid not the slightest attention. "You'll find the president in the reviewing stand. You'll have no trouble in reaching him. Just draw him aside, Professor, and tell him what we've found here. I'll get Dr. Whitaker and the coroner, and Allen here will stay with the body."

I felt a shudder go up my spine, but in another five minutes I saw them all go off, Miss MacIntyre whispering to Miss Chase, Dr. Tyndale looking as if he felt small relish for the task thrust upon him, and Mark Denman very brisk in locking up the doors to the stacks.

There was nothing for me to do except keep watch as I had been ordered to do. In those few harrowing moments while we had stood looking at the body on the floor, Mark Denman had taken command quickly and, I had to admit, in a very efficient manner. It was necessary, of course, for some one to take the lead, and Mr. Denman, as head librarian, was no doubt in the position of responsibility. There seemed to me, however, something rather brusque and almost too hurried in his sudden assumption of authority. He had never questioned that Don's death was an accident. Nor had any of the others. But to me the idea seemed remarkably fantastic. Had the body been found beneath a nineteenth story window or mangled upon railroad tracks, the situation would have been obvious. But that any one could slip on a glass floor and crack his head in such a way as to kill himself seemed altogether too singular.

There was, however, that mark on the floor, that sliding mark which I in my thoughtlessness had placed there. To the others that circumstantial evidence had seemed conclusive. I stood looking down at it now, bitterly regretting the impulse that had prompted my action. But I was not yet ready to confess my deed. The admission would, I could see, put me in the very devil of a fix. I might even be accused of killing my friend and then arranging matters to look accidental. The time for my confession had been when Miss MacIntyre had first called attention to the mark. I had let that opportunity slip. Now I was committed to silence — at least until such time as it became necessary to divulge my secret. I did not dream that before the day was over I should be telling it to President Mittoff.

There was a table in the front aisle, two sections from the space where Don lay. One side of it was against the wall, and at each of the other three sides was a chair. I pulled out one of them preparatory to sitting down. As I did so, my eye caught another glitter on the glass floor near one leg of the table. I stooped to examine it, and I felt the blood pound in my temples at my discovery. Two tiny gold links lay there on the floor. Two tiny gold links!

I thought of the other two I had picked up there by the body before I had carried Agnes Hubbard into the general office. Taking a sheet of yellow paper from one of the table drawers I folded the gold links within it and placed it in my pocket. What could it mean? Two gold links eight feet from the spot where the body lay. And the remarkable thing about it was that, while none of the links showed dust or dirt and must obviously have been dropped there recently, the links were not identical. The last two I had found were much more delicate, much thinner, than the two I had first discovered.

CHAPTER III

I HAD some time to revolve these queries in my mind. It took Mark Denman an unconscionably long time to return. He told me later that he had first tried telephoning the coroner but had learned that he was working that morning on his farm five miles from town, and as there was no telephone at the farmhouse, Denman had driven out for him in his rickety old Ford. Evidently no one was supposed to die that beautiful morning of Alumni Day. Back in town they had stopped at the college infirmary to pick up Dr. Whitaker.

Peering out of the low windows of the stacks, I had occasional glimpses of gaily clad figures hurrying across the open court — bandits, gypsies, barmaids, jockeys, running to take their places in the Alumni procession. Snatches of song blew in the open window:

> "The class of '10
> Had stalwart men
> And lovely lasses
> From all classes
> Of society."

24

The refrain drifted away, and I sat there in the semi-light with a dark cloud of sorrow and suspicion between me and the lovely day.

I suppose I waited there altogether not much longer than thirty or forty minutes, but it seemed an eternity as I sat among those silent books and pondered the situation. Here I was surrounded by the best thoughts, the written meditations of men and women of all ages. But all these recorded words, these thoughts, these fancies, these hypotheses and philosophies were powerless to help me in my present problem. Nor did my own thoughts, trying to cope with the situation, seem of much more avail.

I reviewed the activities of the morning, beginning with the first tap-tap of Agnes Hubbard's heels on the thick green glass of the floor, the sound of a book falling and the soft thud of her body. My first question occurred to me then. What was the book she had taken from the shelf, and what strange chance had sent her to that part of the library the first thing that particular morning?

I rose from the table and walked back to the spot where I had found the girl unconscious on the floor. I remembered clearly that a large book had lain beside her, and I recalled the gap left by the book's removal, that sinister spot of vacancy through which Donald Crawford's hand had dangled. But now there was no gap; every book was in place. Nor could I be sure which volume it was that had been disturbed. I knew which shelf it was, the second one from the bottom. On it were the volumes comprising Frazer's "Golden Bough." I took out one or two of the books, but it seemed a foolish procedure. Even if I held in my hand the correct one, it could offer no clue as to why Agnes Hubbard had removed it. The only explanation of that would be to find the yellow desk slip with the book's number upon it. Some one must certainly have filled out a slip calling for that particular book and have handed it in, signed, to Agnes Hubbard, who had been the only desk girl on duty at that hour. Either that or she had wanted the book herself. I recalled that there had been no one waiting at the desk when I had carried her out of the stacks. The absence of the yellow slip pointed further to the supposition that it was simply a book Agnes Hubbard herself had wished to refer to. But when, during Commencement week, would she have time to read "The Golden Bough"? And who had put the missing book back into place? Well, as far as that went, I might have done so myself. I could not recall the action, but that proved nothing. My mind had received too many shocks in quick succession. I had to leave that question unanswered until I could talk to Agnes Hubbard herself.

I pushed my mind forward to review the reactions of the other four persons who, so far, had viewed the body of Donald Crawford. There was Mark Denman. He had acted just as I would have expected, sincerely horrified. Later he had seemed a little more competent in manner than I would have anticipated, but why blame a man for his ability to rise to the occasion?

Then there was Miss Chase. She had appeared on the scene unexpectedly. But that very unexpectedness might have been expected. Her talents lay in that direction. I could see nothing untoward in her appearing just then. But there were her words to be accounted for. I took from my pocket a notebook and jotted them down as I recalled them. After her first gasp of astonishment she had cried, "Oh, you shouldn't have moved him." That impressed me as being odd now that I thought back on it. How could she know that Denman had turned the body? But Denman had been bending over Don when she came up. It was a natural inference.

But there had been her subsequent confusion. "Of course — of course not — " she had murmured, and then "but — " It was on that word "but" that my mind stuck. Even then I had regretted the interruption of Miss MacIntyre and Dr. Tyndale. Now as I sat alone in the eerie silence and shadows of the stacks, there seemed something ominous back of that one word. I could wrangle nothing significant from it now, however, and I went on to a consideration of Miss MacIntyre and Dr. Tyndale.

Their simultaneous appearance was, no doubt, natural enough. For three years, so the gossips had it, she had been trailing him to and from the university. Personally I read more pathos than humor into her attentiveness. During the past ten years she had made him comfortable in the old colonial house her

father had left her, and where as a girl she had
watched life and youth slip away from her as she
tended a crotchety father and a bed-ridden mother.
If life had later offered her the feeble compensation
of an elderly friendship with an absent-minded old
scholar, I could not find it in my heart to add my
ridicule to that of the town. Though I had lived at
the MacIntyre house during the past year only, I
had witnessed in those months many rather pitiful
examples of the interdependence of these elderly
people. But I could not help wondering what chance
it was that had led them into the stacks that Friday
morning. That would bear investigating, I thought.

Then there were those items I had picked up from
the floor — those two pairs of gold links. I longed to
examine them more closely and to look into the
envelope I had removed from Donald Crawford's
pocket. My fingers closed around the stiff paper,
but I drew them out empty. Far away in a distant
ell of the stacks I heard the stealthy click of a key
and the soft opening of a door. Though the sunlight
was bright in the court outside, though the vivid green
of grass and shrubbery gave evidence of a world of
sanity, I sat stiff in my chair, my eyes glued to that
corner of the stacks toward which the cautious footsteps drew.

The slight suggestion of a chill attacked the region
of my spine, and so great was my relief when the
round fair face of Miss Chase poked itself into the
section where I sat, that I almost burst into a shout
of unseemly laughter.

Finger on lips she approached me. Her large blue eyes darted everywhere at once—at my face, at the windows, down the long aisle, at the shelves of books, at the floor. Ah! I almost breathed aloud the exclamation as I saw her narrowed eyes peer at the floor. The slight squinting of her eyes was, however, the only indication she gave of seeking anything. The rest of her face was immobile in its usual, somewhat childish expression. And if she had been looking for something on the floor, tiny gold links for instance, she immediately relinquished the appearance of hunting as she dropped into a chair beside me.

"Thought you might be lonesome," she remarked, and though she attempted one of her provocative smiles, it ended in something like a grimace as a shiver ran over her. It was hot and close there in the stacks.

"Kind of spooky, isn't it?" Her voice was almost a whisper.

I had to remind myself that it was ten o'clock of a bright June day. "Yes," I replied. "This waiting is no fun. But you needn't share it. How did you get in here anyway?"

"Oh, everyone on the library staff has keys," she answered. "There's only one Bluebeard's chamber in the place. That's the cabinet where the unexpurgated books are kept. Only Mr. Denman has the key to that."

"Yes," I agreed. "I've borrowed that key often. Some of the library's best literature is there."

"While the open shelves sometimes rot with putrefaction," she added.

I was startled at her vehemence. I had not connected that vocabulary with her baby stare. She must have seen the surprise on my face, for she laughed lightly.

"Mr. Denman is a queer one." Her voice seemed woven about a steel core. "Some of the books he recommends for his assistants to read — well — " She shrugged slightly.

This line of conversation seemed to offer no suggestions for continuance. We remained silent a few minutes.

Suddenly she spoke, or rather whispered, and I saw that her eyes had narrowed slightly again. She leaned toward me, laying her hand on my sleeve.

"Have you been through his pockets yet?"

The thin sound of her whisper in that vast abode of books shook me as much as the meaning of her words. I hoped the muscles of my arm had not leaped as had my heart.

"Why should I?" I spoke the words loud enough, but I heard the quiver in my voice, and it was with a conscious effort that I restrained myself from putting my hand in my pocket.

"Oh, I don't know." She was in full possession now of her provocative smile. "Dead men tell no tales, but their pockets sometimes do, and his were usually full enough. You were his best friend. Maybe you know some things that ought to be hidden from a coroner."

"About Don Crawford? His life was an open book." I was indignant, and as I used the hackneyed phrase I had no idea what a sinister overtone that expression must have had to his ghost, had it been lurking in those book-lined lanes.

As if she saw the futility of persuasion, Miss Chase leaped to her feet. "Well, if you won't go through his pockets, I will. He was my friend, too."

She darted down the front aisle, but I had no trouble in catching her before she had touched the body. Her wrists twisted in my grasp, but not until they grew limp did I release her.

"All right, have it your own way," she remarked in quite normal tones. "But don't ever say I didn't warn you."

As she passed the table where we had been sitting, her handkerchief fluttered to the floor. Before I had time to retrieve it, she had stooped. I saw her sweep it across the floor before she lifted it.

"I'm afraid you've got it dirty," I remarked, and I confess that I rather enjoyed the dull flush that crept over her face before she turned and tap-tapped off toward the far ell through which she had come. I listened to the receding steps; I heard the door open and close; the key turned gently.

That young woman knows something, I thought. Then the door on the landing above me opened, and Mark Denman, Dr. Whitaker, and the coroner slowly descended the twelve steps.

CHAPTER IV

WHAT followed was pure routine. Mr. Peppersniff, the sharp-nosed little coroner, expressed small concern or dismay at the tragedy. Just business to him, I thought, as I watched him brush a lock of dark hair back from his eyes as he bent over the body.

Dr. Whitaker spoke a sympathetic word or two in his slow, kindly way, but he wasted no time in making a quick but thorough examination. "Fracture of the skull," he announced. "As you told me, Denman, he must have slipped here, tried to catch himself, and struck his head on one of these braces of the lower shelf."

Mr. Peppersniff added a quick word of agreement.

"Would he have lived long after?" I asked. "I mean if he had been found immediately, would it have been possible to save him?"

"No, death was probably instantaneous. This particular spot at the base of the brain is highly vulnerable."

"Most lamentable misstep." Mr. Peppersniff looked with interest but no pity at the figure on the floor. He turned to Mr. Denman. "Want me to take charge of the body?" Mr. Peppersniff's efficiency combined the morbid offices of coroner and undertaker with the wholesome leaven of farming.

"Perhaps we'd better wait for President Mittoff," suggested Mr. Denman. "Professor Tyndale's gone for him. They should have been here before now."

Even as he spoke we heard footsteps approaching, the unmistakable shuffle of Dr. Tyndale and the firm, heavy stride of President Mittoff. In a second they were beside us.

The countenance of the president was drawn into the stiff anxious lines that his many years of service for Kingsley University had marked about his mouth and eyes. His clothes had their usual appearance of having been thrown on haphazardly. But his fine head and iron gray hair gave him a distinction that no mere carelessness of attire could efface. I had always thought him one of the most conscientious and sympathetic of men, but on that hot June morning, with the activities of another Commencement week goading his hours, he was more abrupt than I had ever seen him. To him, Donald Crawford was just one of the many cogs in his great educational establishment. Under ordinary circumstances he would, I felt, have been more touched by the sadness of the occasion. But in the press of many problems his manner expressed more irritation at the untimeliness of the event than sorrow for the unnecessary death of a promising young man.

He listened to the opinion of Dr. Whitaker and asked about the probable time of death.

"Well," said Dr. Whitaker slowly, pulling at his lower lip with an exasperating deliberateness, "I judge it to have been some time last evening. The body is too cold for death to have occurred this morning. After Mr. Peppersniff and I have examined the body more carefully, I can give you the approximate time."

"How late was the library open last evening?" President Mittoff turned to Mr. Denman.

"Until six o'clock; but of course Mr. Crawford could have entered at any time. All members of the staff have their own keys to the side entrance of the library."

"Oh, certainly." President Mittoff bent his heavy bulk nearer the body of Don Crawford. "It's a frightful accident, especially for such a young man." His words sounded cold and formal.

"Yes, they're plenty of old ones around here whose work is about finished. Isn't that so, Professor?" Mark Denman directed his cruel words straight at Dr. Tyndale.

The old scholar drew himself up erectly. But he said nothing, contenting himself with glaring at Denman. It was an uncomfortable moment, and at the unkind taunt I felt a sudden hatred for Denman flood through me.

The six of us stood there in silence for a moment looking down at the helpless figure. The body had been placed on its back after the coroner's examination of the head. The eyes had been closed, and though the face was peaceful, there was about the mouth a suggestion of mockery, a slight, ironical smile. During the few minutes that President Mittoff, Dr. Whitaker, Mr. Peppersniff and Dr. Tyndale had been there, I had been trying to convince myself that the circumstances were as the others so easily concluded — merely accidental. But now that mocking smile held me. It was not the amazed expression one would expect to find on the face of a person who had lost his balance and who had clutched at a shelf to save himself.

I was about to request a few words alone with President Mittoff, though what I should have said I hardly knew, when he turned to Mr. Denman. "Soft pedal this affair to the press, won't you?" he said. "Publicity of this sort is none too good for the university. I'll have my secretary look up the records of his relatives and notify them."

Undoubtedly it was now time for me to speak. "Crawford had no relatives," I volunteered. "He was an orphan completely alone in the world."

"In that case burial must be in the university plot." President Mittoff turned to me. "You knew Crawford well?"

"As well as any one did."

"Then will you carry out the details of the burial? I have a good many things on my mind these few days. No more of them, I trust, will be of this nature." He frowned slightly, looking at the rest of us as if to forbid our bringing to his attention any more deaths, at least until the turmoil of commencement had subsided.

He bowed slightly and went out followed shortly by Mr. Denman and Dr. Tyndale while I remained a few minutes with Dr. Whitaker and Mr. Peppersniff to discuss details. The coroner assured me that he would see to everything. Burial would be from his parlors at two the next afternoon, if a minister could be obtained. I left, glad of his efficiency, but deeply disturbed by doubts and almost confounded by the strength of my misgivings.

Worried and bewildered, I mounted to the next level and walked into the open rotunda of the library where I saw Agnes Hubbard working again at the filing desk. I stopped for a word of inquiry. She assured me that she was feeling quite all right, but she was very white, and I noticed that her hands shook as she lifted some books onto the counter. Undoubtedly I should, at that moment, have questioned her as to her reason for going to that particular spot in the stacks at precisely nine o'clock, but my mind was on other matters by then, and I hurried to the northeast corner of the rotunda where stairs spiraled upward to the balcony on which Carla Robinson's office was located.

I took the steps two at a time, and I was foolishly out of breath as I saw, through the upper glassed portion of her door, a dark head bent over a stack of papers on the desk. Carla Robinson's power of concentration is superhuman. Though Dr. Tyndale's office is immediately beyond hers, and though he shuffles back and forth a dozen times a day, Carla had told me that only twice had she been conscious of his passing. Then, too, the offices of the student weekly paper, enthusiastically called the *Optima*, are around the bend of the balcony, and while earnest reporters stamped to and from it in constant streams, Carla would work on undisturbed. So now I could not restrain myself from standing for a moment or two outside her door, wondering anew at the clear line of her profile, letting spring flood through my heart again and wash out, momentarily, those past dark hours in the stacks.

Then I knocked. Her head lifted, and the smile that lit up her face was all for me. She would be delighted to go to Collation with me, she said, and wasn't it fine that the Alumni had such a gorgeous day for their antics. By that time my heart was beating a drummer's tattoo against my ribs. But I still had wit enough to know that I must get to my room and examine the contents of my pocket.

"I'll be back for you at twelve-thirty," I announced, my hand on the door knob. But she stopped me.

"What's all the excitement downstairs?" she questioned. "When I came up an hour or so ago Dr. Tyndale and Mr. Denman were having a heated argument, and Miss Chase was coming out of the general office with her arm around Agnes Hubbard. There was something in the air, a sort of hush."

So I told her what had happened, and what Dr. Whitaker had said. And I saw her eyes darken with horror.

"Why it might have been anybody," she cried. "Any one could have slipped on those glass floors.

It might have been — " She paused, but continued commonplacely enough — "anybody."

As I hurried back to my room across the campus gay with costumes, banners, and singing groups, only one question beat in my mind. Had she been about to conclude that sentence with a pronoun of three letters?

CHAPTER V

SPRING had been late that year, and as I turned into the gate of Miss MacIntyre's yard, the heavy fragrance of blossoming locusts enveloped me. In the back garden bluebirds were weaving the air into loops of blue, fastening them with those peculiarly sweet fragments of song that are the very voice of spring. I would have been glad to linger in the garden where I saw old Miss MacIntyre poking about with a cane, but my fingers itched to examine the contents of my pocket.

I hardly knew what I expected to find. That jagged tear in the envelope was so uncharacteristic of Don Crawford. My curiosity was at a high pitch. But had I allowed my imagination the widest possible range, I could not have guessed at the contents that I spread out on the desk before me. It was a letter written in long hand on an ordinary sheet of typewriter paper. Black ink had been used, and the writing was in a round regular hand. There had obviously been no attempt to disguise it. The letter was signed quite clearly. I read it with complete amazement.

"DEAREST,

Although I could kill you, I still address you in the old way. Odd, isn't it? This is to tell you, since you no longer allow me to speak to you, that I will not endure the situation much longer. I know all about your present affair. I was a fool ever to keep our marriage secret. I was so much a fool that at first I even thought it fun. But I will not submit to seeing you make love to some one else under my very eyes. I give you this opportunity to talk things over with me within the next three days. At the end of that time, if you have made no move to see me, I shall take matters into my own hands.

I am still fool enough to love you.

BERTHA."

When I use the words "complete amazement" to describe my reaction to the letter, I am doing slight justice to the utter stupefaction I then felt. Don Crawford and Bertha Chase! I could imagine no more poorly mated couple. No wonder the envelope had been hastily torn. Don must have known from whom it came. It had not been sent through the mails. The envelope bore no line of writing. I had a sudden vision of Bertha Chase tipping on her ridiculous heels past Don's desk, dropping the envelope and walking nonchalantly on.

So they had been secretly married. How long ago and where, I wondered. I recalled clearly that she had occasionally followed him about the library and had turned her fervid gaze upon him rather frequently. I had razzed him about it on one or two occasions, and he had taken my teasing with more annoyance than I would have expected. No word or attitude of his had given indication of a possible affection. He had indeed kept the secret well.

No wonder Bertha Chase had returned to the stacks this morning. No wonder she had suggested searching Don's pockets. That opening clause leered up at me from the page, "Although I could kill you — " But the conclusion was contradictory: "I am still fool enough to love you." Suddenly it became imperative for me to determine just when that note had been written. It had given him three days' grace. Then, it had said: "I shall take matters into my own hands." To-day was Friday. Don Crawford had died Thursday evening. By some means I must determine if that note had been written before Monday.

I felt as though weeks had passed since I had walked up the tree-lined streets toward George and Harry's. But a glance at my watch told me it had been less than five hours. I still had forty-five minutes before it was time for me to be back at Carla Robinson's office. I had formed no plan of procedure when I ran down the curving stairs of Miss MacIntyre's house, but I directed my steps toward the library. The Alumni procession was breaking up as I hurried across the campus, and I was detained three or four times by the hearty greetings of old students who had been "out in the world" two or three years and who seemed amazed to find me still active and mentally unimpaired.

A glance into the general office told me that it

would be useless to start my activities there. Mr. Denman was directing a bevy of beautiful co-eds in the difficult task of pasting and varnishing labels on books. An interruption at such a moment would have netted me less than nothing.

As it chanced, however, fortune smiled on me, though smiled is not, perhaps, the best term to employ. For there was nothing but agitation in the manner with which Agnes Hubbard beckoned me toward her desk.

"I've just remembered," she began. "Mr. Crawford entrusted something to me yesterday which I think I'd better turn over to you."

Before I had time to reply, the bright smile of Bertha Chase was playing on us as she teetered past toward the filing drawers.

"I have to look up a book in the stacks," I said in a conversational tone. And with this subtle hint I disappeared into those twilit lanes. In a few moments Agnes Hubbard joined me, looking trim and capable but very anxious.

"Let's go down to the basement level," she said. "There's sure to be no one in the old magazine section at this time of day."

So down the two flights of steel stairs we made our way. She insisted on going up and down all the aisles to make certain we were alone before she finally led me to the most remote corner. It was a spot exactly one floor below the place where Don Crawford's body had lain. But the macabre coincidence did not seem to occur to her. A table was pushed against the wall with two or three chairs near it. She sank into one of these. I noticed that her face was very pale, and that beneath her gray eyes dark smudges extended down into her cheeks. I wondered if it was work only that brought that look of utter fatigue to her face. This was the end of her Junior year, and she had maintained an A average in all her classes, at the same time working her way through college. Perhaps she had driven herself beyond her strength with her peculiar mind, at once naïvely questioning and penetratingly alert. I thought of that strange blend now as she turned her eyes so full of lights and shadows upon me. She seemed to wait for me to make the first move.

"Well, let's see what it is that was entrusted to you," I said.

"Oh, I haven't it with me. I wouldn't touch it again now that Don — that Mr. Crawford is dead." She shuddered. "It's hidden. You'll have to get it yourself."

I must admit that I was beginning to feel impatient. The girl's sensibilities seemed to me rather too delicate. My irritation was apparently evident, for she sat up very straight, looking directly at me, and said with great dignity, "It's all a little queer. I thought I'd better tell you about it first. You see I'm afraid it's valuable."

"But what is it? Don didn't have anything valuable," I began. But even as I denied it, I recalled again his remark of the preceding day, "I believe I've got hold of something valuable." Why had this thing, whatever it was, been committed to the care of Agnes Hubbard?

"Wait till I tell you the circumstances." She glanced nervously down the long book-lined aisle before she continued. Her hands were clenched on the table before her, the vividly painted nails biting into her palm. A false note, those nails, I thought, as she began her story.

Don had come to her, it seemed, on the afternoon of the preceding day and asked her if she could keep something for him, something that he didn't want to carry around with him. "I think it's worth something," he had said, "and it's worth something to some one else besides me. Can you lock it away for me?" Yes, she had told him, she could. She had a desk in an upstairs alcove where she did some of her cataloguing.

"There's a secret drawer in it, Mr. Allen," she said, her eyes wide and serious as they rested on my face. "It's one of those ordinary office desks with a lot of little cubby holes in front and a small drawer between them. When you pull out the center drawer there's a flat surface that looks like the back of the desk. But it isn't the back. It's just a thin piece of wood. And if you slide a knife in one end of it, it flies open and there's a space about six by eight inches. I found it accidentally when I was trying to dig out some dirt from around the edges. Mr. Crawford said that was the very place."

"But what did he give you? What was this valuable thing?"

She looked about her again nervously. "Listen!"
she said. "Did you hear something just then?"

I looked off into the dim alley ways. Only books
and a faint green light reflected from the shrubbery
outside the low windows met my eyes, and only the
silence of printed words fell about my ears.

"There's nothing," I assured her. "You're only
excited."

"Well," she said, "I don't suppose you'll believe
me, but I don't know what it was he gave me."

"You don't know?"

"No, it was in an envelope. I didn't even touch it.
He put it in the desk himself." She tapped her
brilliant nails nervously on the table.

"But you saw the envelope?"

"Yes, it was just a plain manila envelope. We
use hundreds of them in the library every week.
You see, I never thought of it again till just a few
minutes ago. Then somehow I didn't want to touch
it. I couldn't bear to, with him lying dead. And
I was just wondering what I ought to do when you
came into the library."

"You have done exactly right," I told her. "Come
on, we'll see if the coast's clear and we'll get it
immediately."

She led the way upstairs. It was by then twelve-
thirty, and every one had left for the lower campus
where Collation was being served. Every one except
one person in her office on the balcony. I hoped she
was still waiting.

The rotunda was deserted. Agnes Hubbard took

me to the alcove where her desk stood. It was a plain
oak affair, rather shabby, and it certainly bore no
air of mystery.

"You open it," she said pointing to the small
center drawer. "I don't want to touch it."

I pulled out the small drawer, and she handed
me an open penknife, directing me where to insert it.
The action of the spring was exactly as she had
described it. The thin piece of wood snapped outward, disclosing the hidden aperture. My hand was
already poised to reach inside, but it remained poised
there in the air above the desk. The small opening
was completely empty.

My first feeling was that the whole thing was a
fairy tale. It had all sounded a bit too fantastic.
But Agnes Hubbard's gasp assured me there was
reality to the situation. "It's gone," she whispered,
her voice as hollow as that small opening in her
desk. Then she began to cry.

"Are you sure it was there?" I asked unsympatheti-
cally. I could have found no better way to stem the
flood of tears. My question angered her.

"Of course I'm sure. I saw him put it there."

"Then it must have slipped down a crack," I
replied, shoving my fingers into the opening. But
there was no crack through which even the thinnest
piece of paper might have disappeared.

The tears were about to start forth afresh when I
faced her. "Now see here, what was this envelope
like?" I asked her. "How big was it?"

I watched her stiffen in an effort to control herself. "Oh, it wasn't big," she answered. "Just one

of those ordinary letter envelopes, three and a half by six and a half, I think."

"But how did it look?" I persisted. "Can't you recall one thing about it? Was it lumpy in one corner as if it contained jewelry? Or was it thin?"

She shut her eyes a minute. "No," she said firmly, "it wasn't any of those things. I can remember perfectly how it looked. It was fat. Bulky, as if it had papers folded up inside it. It didn't look valuable at all."

I looked again at the drawer and into the small opening. There was no place where a bulky envelope could accidentally have lodged.

"We'll have to look further," I said. "But it's twenty minutes to one now, and I have an engagement."

"It's been stolen. I'm sure of it," she answered.

I had a sudden flash of thought. "Perhaps not. Perhaps he came back and got it last night before he was mur — before he died."

She grew very pale. "Oh, you think, too, that he was killed?"

"Miss Hubbard, I must talk to you again soon." My voice sounded portentous even in my own ears. "At that same table in the basement stacks at five this afternoon?"

She nodded mutely.

I took the steps three at a time this trip, and I discovered that Carla Robinson is possessed either of angelic patience or the most guileful femininity, for all she said to my apologies was, "Oh, is it late? I've been so busy I never noticed."

CHAPTER VI

THE luncheon in the lower campus proved to be the usual picnic meal that all colleges serve on such occasions, fruit salad, potato chips and sandwiches, followed by ice cream and cake. But with Carla Robinson beside me I might have been dining on the delicacies of a French *cuisine*. And in her laughter I forgot the past dark hours.

"Peer Gynt" was being given in the open air theatre that afternoon. We watched it for an hour, though I looked at the audience and at Carla as much as at the actors, and my mind was following more closely problems of my own than the sorrows of Solveig. At our right, looking pert but a trifle tense, Miss Chase sat with Miss Leighton, a rotund lady of middle age who had charge of a rooming house where I had lived for four years. I noticed a worried little frown on Miss Chase's forehead, and I thought how much more deeply those lines would be etched if she but knew that locked away in my desk was the letter she had wanted so much to retrieve. Agnes Hubbard was there too, looking rested and pretty in a pink dress. She was accompanied by a Senior named

Benjamin Morris, who had been editor of the *Optima* throughout the past year. Propinquity in the library had, no doubt, brought them together. Farther back, Mr. Denman was enjoying himself between two co-eds, Polly Sanderson, a red-haired beauty, and Betty Murchison, a brunette of no less pulchritude. Well to the front President Mittoff sat surrounded by trustees. His wife had died during the past year, and I knew how sorely he must miss her graciousness on occasions such as this. She had taken many of the social burdens from his shoulders. Despite his morning brusqueness I felt a flood of sympathy for the man.

Much as I should have liked to spend the afternoon exactly where I was, I felt it necessary to make a visit to the undertaker's. Carla elected to leave the play with me, and together we sauntered back across the tree-shaded campus.

I was not particularly good company, I knew, for while half my mind was savoring the enchantment of the hour, the other half was pounding down blind alleys of wonder and suspicion. Carla interrupted a particularly long silence by what I thought was a very pertinent observation, though probably my abstraction was obvious enough.

"Tom, you're worried, aren't you? Can I help any?"

I had intended to keep my own counsel in the entire affair, but her question broke my resolve immediately. The fact also that she had an office in the library assumed a sudden significance. She might be able to throw light on some of the points that were puzzling me.

"I am worried," I admitted. "I ought not to tell you, but I shall. I have very scant evidence to the contrary, but I can't convince myself that Don Crawford's death was accidental."

"You don't think it was accidental! What do you mean?"

"I mean just this — that I have a strong suspicion that he was murdered."

She gave a low cry. "But how could he have been? He had no enemies surely. Who could have done it?"

"That's just what I must find out. At present I haven't the slightest idea. But I have a few leads, and I'm going after them. Maybe you could help me with one or two."

She shivered, but her voice was firm. "Why, of course, I'll do anything I can. What a terrible thing! Oh, I do think you are wrong."

"I hope so. The next few days will determine that. Tell me, how could I find out when the ink was last changed in the library?"

"One of the student assistants, Helen Gardner, tends to all that," she replied. "When any one in the building wants ink, or paper, or supplies of any sort he makes out a requisition and gives it to Helen Gardner. She fills the order from the supply room."

I had a momentary picture of myself quizzing Helen Gardner. It would be awkward. I should have to make an opportunity. Probably some one would see me questioning her, or she might talk about it afterward.

"Do you know this Helen Gardner well?" I asked Carla.

"Yes, as it happens, I do. She's had poor training in French, and she hasn't much money. I've been giving her a little extra time to coach her along."

"If you asked her some rather odd questions could you rely on her to be discreet?"

"She'd do anything for me," Carla said impulsively. Then she blushed charmingly. "I mean she's grateful."

"I'd be grateful, too," I replied, "if you'd get in touch with her, then. Perhaps I'd do anything for you, too."

There was mild reproach in her glance, but no anger. "Well, what am I to ask her?"

"Just this. Ask her to show you all her requisition blanks for the past ten days. Copy out everything on them for me. Dates, supplies requested, by whom, and anything else the blanks contain. Make up any excuse to Helen Gardner that you want to. But do get the information."

"I can give it to you this evening," she told me. "Helen's coming to my office at eight to go over her exam paper with me. By nine o'clock I can have both tasks accomplished."

"I could kiss you," I said. But I didn't. I left her at the steps of the library and dashed off toward Mr. Peppersniff's establishment, my cheeks more flushed than her own. In fact she looked quite cool.

Mr. Peppersniff led me to his office. "Everything's going well," he told me. "I have a bunch of letters and papers here that we took from the pockets." He handed them to me. "Got the minister all right for to-morrow — Dr. Tressel. Be here by two o'clock. Suppose there won't be many for the funeral — such a busy time."

"No, just a few friends," I assured him. "Have you looked over the — " I hesitated.

"Yes, we're working on him now." He understood my hesitancy. I suppose at such times he has to read between the lines of a good many remarks.

"Doc Whitaker examined him thoroughly. Put the time of death between eight and nine o'clock. Young man hit his head good and hard all right. Shattered the atlas and axis. Pierced the medulla oblongata just as Doc Whitaker said this morning. Bruise under his chin, too. Must have struck a shelf trying to catch himself."

"I'd like to see that bruise," I said.

He gave me a quick look and led the way to his laboratory. His assistant, working in a matter-of-fact way over the body which lay stretched on a table, paid little attention to me as I stepped up to the body. Against the shrunken pallor of the face, drained now of its blood, was a small bruise, slightly discolored beneath the curve of the chin. It could indeed have been caused, as Mr. Peppersniff suggested, by contact with a shelf, but later as I walked down the street I told myself that it could have come also from a good stiff whack on the chin delivered by a less inanimate object than a steel shelf. A blow at the base of the brain might have knocked him forward. Equally well could a punch on the chin have knocked him backward. It was baffling. The position in which we had found him indicated that he had gone down on his side. It did not, in any way, account for the bruise on his chin.

I felt, however, that now if ever I should carry my suspicions to President Mittoff. Accordingly I stopped in at the dignified white brick house that is his home. I was fortunate in catching him just as he was returning from the play, and, although he was accompanied by several members of the board of trustees, he allowed me ten minutes of his time. Settled in his cool, high-ceilinged study, I made my remarks as brief as possible, though I did not gloss over the fact that, to my mind, the circumstances were serious. One of the greatest assets of President Mittoff is his ability to give his complete attention to the matter in hand. To a man in an administrative position of any sort this power to comprehend and judge swiftly is an invaluable asset. So now, busy as he was with social and academic affairs, he listened with complete absorption while I told the story of my doubts, of my experimental slide on the glass floor, of the strange loss of the envelope concealed in Agnes Hubbard's desk. Of the minor details I made no mention. There was no time, and it seemed unnecessary to allude to matters which, like Bertha Chase's letter, might have no bearing on the case.

President Mittoff frowned once or twice during

my recital, and I saw a swift smile pass across his face as I related the unfortunate interpretation placed upon my slide on the glass floor. I felt that my story was not very convincing. The mere putting of it into words made it seem like the extravagant phantasy of a prying old maid. And while the president appeared to give serious consideration to my words, on the whole he seemed rather unimpressed.

"I don't know what to say to you, Allen," he remarked as I concluded my story. "There doesn't seem much to go on, not enough to warrant our getting in a detective. If there's nothing in it, the publicity would be a bad thing for us. How would it strike you if I turned over any investigation you might think necessary to you yourself? Would you be willing to undertake it? If you come across any actual proof that Crawford met with foul play, it would then be time to call in the authorities."

We left it at that. I felt relieved now that I had carried my suspicions to some one higher in authority. President Mittoff evidently thought I was making a mountain out of a mole hill. But what if I were not? Could I but have known the volcanic nature of that mountain and the series of dire occurrences that were about to flow over us, I should not have raced so blithely up the library steps to keep my appointment with Agnes Hubbard.

There was one question puzzling me, and I reminded myself that I must immediately inquire about it. The only persons visible in the library were a few visitors wandering about the halls and reading rooms.

I hurried to the basement stacks where Agnes Hubbard was already waiting. Immediately I propounded my question.

"How was it," I asked, "that you happened to go to that particular corner of the library so early this morning?"

She looked at me oddly, a worried frown on her forehead.

To jog her memory I continued, "You had taken a book from the shelves. Was it one you wanted for yourself, or had some one turned in a request slip for it?"

She glanced nervously about. "I promised I wouldn't tell," she said finally.

"But it's important," I urged her. "It's strange, too. There couldn't have been many people wanting books so early on Alumni Day. And I don't remember seeing any one about when I carried you up from the stacks."

"I know," she said, and I felt that she had resolved to break her promise. "I thought it was strange, too. Maybe if I wrote the name of the person on a piece of paper, that wouldn't be exactly telling."

I have never had any patience with such a childish evasion of sincerity, but as she looked at me questioningly, I nodded my head. It was no time for an ethical quibble.

She grasped in her brightly colored finger tips the pencil I held out to her and wrote on a sheet of yellow paper two words — Miss Chase.

I tore the paper into fragments and put them in

my pocket. "Why didn't she get it herself?" I asked.

"Oh, she often asks me to get books for her when she's busy. It's part of my job, you know."

"But when did she ask you not to tell?" I questioned. "And why?"

"It was later when I'd recovered from my faint. She said it might look funny, and as it was only a coincidence she'd rather I didn't say anything about it."

So that was why Bertha Chase had put her arm around Agnes Hubbard as they came out of the general office. It was that very scene that Carla Robinson had witnessed.

I stored the girl's words in my memory. "Thank you very much," I said. "And just one other question. What makes you think Don Crawford's death was not accidental? Why do you think he was killed?"

A deep flush dyed her cheeks. The shadows in her eyes deepened. Back of those shadows, I knew, lurked thoughts she had no intention of revealing. She laughed nervously. "Oh, I don't know. I guess I was excited when I said that. It just didn't seem possible at first that any one could have fallen that hard."

She gave me a quick, penetrating look. "But you thought so, too. You were about to say, this morning, that he had been murdered."

Inwardly I cursed that slip of the tongue, but I was resolved to make light of it. "I know," I said. "I guess we were both excited. That dangling hand must have given us both the jitters. And anyway we saw the place where he slipped." For once I could turn that mistake of mine into an advantage.

"Yes," she said doubtfully. "But any one could have made that mark. You might have yourself."

The advantage seemed decidedly on her side. I wondered if she had been unconscious all the time she lay there on the floor. But I knew that she had been. Her remark had been only a chance hit. But it had changed our positions somewhat. I felt disinclined to pursue the subject at that moment. At some later time perhaps I could catch her off guard.

"Come," I said. "We'd better search that desk more thoroughly now."

She smiled, and all the shadows in her eyes changed into lights as she accompanied me to the alcove.

There were only a few strangers about as we went upstairs and through the rotunda. The library seemed sufficiently empty for our purpose. Every part of the desk was subjected to our scrutiny, not a difficult task to accomplish, for the drawers and pigeonholes were in almost perfect order. Nothing more exciting than clips, filing cards, stickers, papers and the like rewarded our searching. In a last vain attempt I got to my hands and knees and crawled into the center space which was like a dark cave between the two rows of large drawers through which we had been searching. It was when I was in this undignified position that I heard footsteps. Before I could extricate myself the satiric voice of Mr. Denman greeted my ears.

"Lost your collar button, Mr. Allen?" he inquired.

I crawled out to find him grinning broadly at me. Beside him stood Dr. Tyndale peering nearsightedly at my position and murmuring rather ineffectually, "Dear me, dear me, you *are* rather dusty, Dr. Allen." He brushed me off with surprising vigor while Mr. Denman merely stood there with an amused smile on his face.

"I was — er — looking for a manuscript Miss Hubbard is typing for me," I explained rather lamely. "The last page seems to be lost."

Agnes Hubbard cast a reproachful glance at me. Neatness is one of her virtues, and I suppose she cherishes her reputation for it. But she played up to my lie very well, for when I turned toward her and said with an effort of casualness, "Never mind about it then, Miss Hubbard. I'll rewrite it from my notes," she replied in a subdued tone, "Thank you very much. I'm sorry I lost it."

As I took my way homeward, slowing my steps to match those of Dr. Tyndale, I blessed the girl for her quick wit, and I thanked Heaven that the affair had passed off with so little question. I did not dream that my next visit to the library was to be fruitful of surprises and that I was to find, not the missing article, but some one nearer to death than most of us ever come without entirely reaching it.

Our progress across the campus was halted many times as students of bygone days stopped to exchange a word with Dr. Tyndale. He had been thirty years at Kingsley University, and his kindly scholasticism and absent-mindedness had endeared him to many students during those years.

"It makes one feel a patriarch," he said when we finally strolled up the fragrant path to Miss MacIntyre's house. "Years ago when I was a student in Germany, I used to regard my professors with reverence. But now all I revere is old books."

I thought of his large collection of books, none of them rare, but many of them fine and well-chosen. It was rumored that they were all willed to the university, and I wondered if life had in store for me such a dusty destiny.

CHAPTER VII

F OR the next hour I sat at my desk going over carefully the letters and papers that Mr. Peppersniff had gathered together from Don Crawford's pockets. There were some twenty envelopes, all torn neatly at one end. I sorted them into three piles: bills; orders and receipts for books, both English and American; and the usual mimeographed university notices and communications. In the entire lot there was nothing personal. Apparently my chance discovery of the letter from Bertha Chase was the only communication of special interest in the entire collection. Strange that I had come upon it so immediately.

As I came down the stairs on my evening trip to George and Harry's my nostrils were filled with the delicious smell of frying chicken. Perhaps, after all, life was not such a lonely affair for an old pedagogue, I mused. It had long been Miss MacIntyre's habit to share her evening meal with Dr. Tyndale. On very special occasions during the past year I had been asked to join them, and at such times I felt like a prodigal son returned to the old homestead after far wanderings. A spirit of gentle comradeship existed between these two old people which at such times made me feel that they were happier together than are many an elderly couple who have shared all life's joys and vicissitudes together.

Dr. Tyndale's small Scotty was waddling about the lawn with great dignity as I let myself out of the house. Books, a dog, and a gentle lady to take care of one. Surely I need feel no sympathy for my old housemate.

On my way to dinner I stopped in at Don Crawford's rooming house. It took me only ten minutes to learn that there was nothing important there. The place was as bare as a hermit's cell. What few clothes Don had were hanging neatly in the closet. In his desk I found only a bank book with regular entries, and a check book, the stubs of which revealed nothing except that Don's only extravagance was books, which he purchased in both New York and England. The latest order had been from Craig & Bainbridge and the stub read $30.00. I smiled to recall that it was more than Don had ever spent for a suit of clothes.

The marriage certificate that I had hoped, or feared, to find was nowhere in evidence. No doubt Bertha Chase had retained possession of it. There was, in fact, nothing in the room which gave indication of characteristics other than the very admirable ones I had always known my friend to possess. I closed the door quietly and went on my way.

The pork chops at George and Harry's seemed

particularly uninspired that evening, and the customers looked unusually wilted. After the meal I fell in with two boys back for their first reunion and listened to their hard luck tales of depression idleness as we walked back toward the university. I had intended to return to my room to complete the grading of my final examination papers; but the evening was warm, and the groups of pleasant people persuaded me to linger and listen to the Senior Sing on the steps of Webb Hall. Deep and plaintive melodies swelled out across the campus, one of the sentimental and yet genuine expressions of a group of youngsters who had worked and played together through four years of what we choose to call "opportunity." Now that the day of parting was imminent they felt the bond more strongly than ever before. The minor notes of their songs drifted across the twilit campus, and I thought of Don Crawford whose farewell to it all had been so unexpected and so final. It was with a rather grim determination that I took the path to the library as the chapel clock tolled out the hour of nine.

I saw lights in Carla's office as I neared the library, and I wished that I had asked her to be at the main door of the building to admit me. I did not exactly relish the idea of making use of one of the windows opening into the basement stacks. I tried the four doors to the building, the front one, the entrances on both sides and a basement entrance at the rear east. All of them were secure. I looked around a bit for the night-watchman of the campus, old Emil Schlachtman, but he was nowhere to be seen. From

the darkness of a tree his enormous dog, looking like
the shadow of a lean beast, leaped past me, followed
by the small Scotty. But of Emil I could find no
trace, nor could I see the glimmer of his flashlight
about any of the near buildings. I gave up hunting
for him as a bad business. He might be in any of a
hundred places. Reluctantly I returned to the rear of
the building and parted the bushes that grew in a
dense mass outside the windows. I raised the window and stepped silently in.

Within this section of the library darkness hung
in thick curtains. Cautiously I took a few steps.
Suddenly above me I heard muffled footsteps. They
receded, but instead of fading away entirely, they
came to a sudden halt. Then a light flashed on. A
thrill ran to my very fingertips when I realized that
it was near the section where Don Crawford's body
had been discovered. There was complete silence for
a moment, then a quick sliding noise as when a book
is removed from a tightly packed shelf.

Certainly none of these sounds was suspicious. The
person above me had quite openly turned on the
lights for his task. I marked the illuminated section.
Throughout the stacks every other case has at its
end a button which illuminates the section between
two shelves. The portion now lighted was not at the
extreme end. It was nearer the center staircase, two
sections from the west wall. I told myself that Carla
Robinson was probably up there in search of a book,
but something else told me that she would never
venture along those ghost-like alleyways in the dark,

especially since I had that afternoon acquainted her with my suspicions. One part of my mind told me that nothing untoward was going on above me, but that other part which had all day filled me with doubts and suspicions led me forward on tiptoe. The darkness was intense, but, feeling my way from shelf to shelf, I neared the staircase, determined to mount them and see with my own eyes who the intruder was.

Unexpectedly my knee encountered a chair. There was a sharp grating noise as it slid over the glass floor. Instantly the light above me was extinguished. That at least told me something. Interruption was not desired. Regardless now of the darkness, I dashed forward. As I found the staircase, I heard feet pounding along the upper floor. And before I had reached the second level, I heard them mounting to the third and then to the fourth. An overturned chair met me at the top of the first flight and sent me sprawling. My adversary (as I now thought of him) was a clever strategist. Above, all was silence. I could picture him standing at the top of the fourth flight, waiting. And as I had no desire to feel a heavy book descend on my cranium, I felt my way to the exit leading to the rotunda. The library was plunged into darkness save where lights from Carla's and the student publications' office lit up the balcony. I ascended the curving stairs and stood in Carla's doorway. She was alone, and reading in a rather desultory fashion, for she looked up immediately upon my appearance.

She had done better with the requisition slips than I had expected. She had persuaded Helen Gardner to leave them with her, promising to put them back herself in their proper file. Moreover, one of the requisitions had seemed unusual. She had asked some questions about it. I could scarcely hide my excitement when she pulled out that slip. On the date line was written "June 4th" (which had been Monday); and under the column headed ARTICLES, there were listed "100 paper clips", "one bottle of ink — black." The word "black" had been underlined. The handwriting was round and regular, and the signature read "Bertha Chase."

"It was the word 'black' I asked about," said Carla. "You see the ink we usually use here is blue."

"Could Helen Gardner give any explanation?"

"Yes, she could. She said the books that needed mending were being collected now. There's a special filing system in connection with that work, and black ink is always used. Here's a card with Mr. Denman's signature. You see, he asked for black ink that same day."

"And blue had been in use until then?"

"Yes, Helen was sure of that because she hadn't had any requests for black ink since Christmas. She had to go to the general university storeroom to fill this order."

We went through the other requisitions, but they seemed ordinary enough. Yellow paper, clips, filing cards, manila envelopes, pencils, pens, blue books for both Carla and Dr. Tyndale, stamped envelopes

for the student publications' offices. There were only
two slips to hold the attention, those of Bertha Chase
and Mr. Denman, both dated omiously enough June
4th. And for me, only that of the woman held any
significance. In itself it was unexceptional, but
coupled with the letter I had found in Don's pocket
it had sinister implications.

"I shall give you this opportunity to talk things
over with me within the next three days," she had
written in bold, black ink. "At the end of that time,
if you have made no move to see me, I shall take
matters into my own hands." Thursday had been
the third day, and it was that evening that Don
Crawford had come to his death.

A wave of almost physical illness swept over me as
I realized how infallibly the two and two I had put
together made four. I had never liked Bertha Chase
with her baby blue eyes, her mincing steps and provocative manner; but there was a helpless quality
about the girl that made me loath to call her, even to
my own mind, a murderer.

I sighed. "Well, you have given me an invaluable
clue," I told Carla. "And now if you know where
these cards belong, we'd better return them."

Carla locked her office door. The balcony was dark
save for the patches of light that shone out from the
two doors leading to the offices of the *Optima.*
Several students were there, supposedly cleaning up
and destroying old copy, but they seemed to be doing
more laughing than working. Their voices echoed
gaily through the vast dark rotunda. I thought for

a moment of the dark stacks and of the figure that, at my approach, had fled upward. What sudden contrasts this building presented! Perhaps I should have done better to pursue that shadowy shape. Where was it lurking now? I snapped on a light on the balcony and pushed another button that controlled the great chandelier overhanging the rotunda. Then we started down the vast well of the spiral staircase. The memory of my previous encounter had robbed me of any desire to plunge into unknown depths of blackness.

We had gone down only about seven steps of the rather long flight when, with no warning signal, the entire building was thrown into complete darkness. The light on the balcony, the great chandelier, the illumination in the *Optima* offices were all succeeded by that sudden density of darkness which is always so much more impenetrable when one's eyes are adjusted to any light, however faint.

Instantly we halted there on the stairs, and my hand sought and found Carla's. I did not think till afterward how confidently her fingers had closed about mine.

"It must be ten o'clock," she said. "All the lights go out then. They're turned off at the power house."

I am a poor judge of time when I am in her presence, but I felt that the hour could not be so late. Before I had time to answer, a loud crash came from below us. Then utter silence.

"The switch box, where is it?" I demanded, clutching Carla's fingers tightly in my own.

"To the right of the main desk." Her voice was steady, but her hand went cold in my clasp.

"Go back to your office. Lock yourself in, and don't budge till I come for you," I said.

Then quietly I felt my way to the bottom of the staircase. The rotunda was a vast, dark cave before me, but I had crossed it often enough to be sure of my direction. I had no difficulty in reaching the main desk, shaped in a large semicircle, and by it I guided myself to the right toward the back wall. So far no sound had succeeded the first loud crash. But now my ears caught distinctly the sound of low moans farther to my right. I reached out my hand in an attempt to locate the switch box. It touched — not the cold wall I had expected — but the harsh serge of a man's sleeve. I felt the arm jerk from beneath my fingers. All about me there seemed to be furtive movement. I could distinguish the quick breathing of two persons. I threw my arms out wildly, trying to clutch again at that serge coat There was a sharp click. The steel door of the switch box banged to, and at the same time a quick blow sent me staggering backward. As I regained my balance I heard again the heavy pounding of feet in the stacks. It sounded like an army. At the same instant there came from without the building the hollow baying of Emil's great dog.

The switch box was now locked, and for a second I stood there catching my breath. Then beside me I heard a whisper. It was Carla.

"I followed you," she breathed. "Who shut the switch box?"

"If I only knew," I answered, fumbling for my match box. But it was empty.

"I think I can find the key." Carla's whisper was close to my ear, and taking my hand she led me behind the desk. "I've seen Agnes Hubbard put it in a drawer here," she said. She fumbled about in the drawers a moment or two. In another second she pressed the cold metal into my hand. I found the box and threw the switch. The lights in the chandelier and on the balcony flashed on. Carla pressed one or two buttons on the main floor.

By that time, of course, my assailant had escaped. Pursuit would be futile. I had been foiled twice within the hour. And now there were those low moans off to our right. Some one was lying there hurt, perhaps dying. I had given no thought as to who it might be. But now I realized that the sounds came from the alcove where Agnes Hubbard and I had searched so ineffectually both morning and afternoon. Was the girl lying there now seriously injured? Carla and I hastened toward the sound, switching on another light as we went.

There by the desk, crumpled in a heap on the floor, her eyes closed, her light hair matted with blood, lay Bertha Chase.

CHAPTER VIII

HAD I had time to form any expecta-
tions of whom I should find sprawled on the floor of
the alcove, the last person I should have thought
of would have been Bertha Chase. She presented a
ghastly spectacle doubled up on the floor beside the
overturned desk chair. All the color had drained from
her face, and blood was pouring down her forehead
and across one colorless cheek. Carla lifted the blond
hair from one side of her head, revealing a long
bloody gash. I looked at it unbelievingly for a moment, and in that brief breath of time something else
caught my attention. One hand of the unconscious
girl was clenched around an envelope, a plain manila
envelope about three and a half by six and a half
inches. I loosened the fingers and stuffed it in my
pocket.

As I lifted her I thought how similarly the day
was ending as it had begun for me. At nine that
morning I had stuffed an envelope into my pocket
and had carried the limp form of Agnes Hubbard
out of the stacks. Now, at a few minutes before ten
in the evening, a second envelope was in my pocket

and I held another lax figure in my arms. But I knew that this was no ordinary faint. A little water dashed in the face of this girl would not revive her.

By this time several boys from the *Optima* offices had come racing down the stairs.

"Miss Chase had a fall in the dark," I told them. "I think we'd better take her to the infirmary."

Carla made a temporary bandage of several handkerchiefs the boys provided. Then I chose four boys to carry the unconscious girl over to Maple Street where the college hospital is located. Carla and I followed.

Over by Webb Hall we could see the glimmer of Japanese lanterns and groups of people still lingering to exchange reminiscences and experiences. I spoke in low tones to Carla.

"I'm going to ask something further of you," I said. "And it's not something easy this time. If the nurse will let you, I wish you'd stay with Miss Chase all night. Above all, don't go to sleep. And listen carefully to everything she says."

I fished an address book and pencil from my pocket. "Here," I said, "take these. And if you have a chance jot down anything she says. She may talk when she's regaining consciousness. It's important that we know exactly what she says."

"Do you think they'll let me stay?" Carla's voice sounded breathless.

"Yes. They'll have to let you. I'll tell them you're one of her best friends."

"But I'm not, you know. I scarcely know the girl."

"Well, keep that under your hat. If I'm any judge of appearances, that girl won't be rational enough to recognize anybody for several days."

"Do you want me to stay all that time?"

"No, I'm not going to make you a prisoner. But if she regains consciousness to-night she may say something important. Something about what she was doing there in that alcove and who it was that hit her."

"If she knows," Carla said. "She probably doesn't know any more about it than we do. She can't see in the dark any better than we can."

"Well, it's worth a chance. Are you willing?"

"Of course I am. But it's rather like eavesdropping, isn't it?"

"Perhaps. But it's important. Deucedly important," I added as I remembered the manila envelope in my pocket. That envelope was empty. I could tell that much in the second I had slipped it into my pocket.

By that time we had reached the infirmary. I rang the bell, and, when one of the nurses came, held the door open as the boys carried their limp burden into the hallway.

"Miss Chase had a fall in the library," I said.

The nurse, Miss Johnson, a thoroughly capable person in the middle thirties, led the way down the left corridor and switched on a light in one of the rooms. Accustomed as she is to seeing boys brought in unconscious from the football field, she looked at that moment rather frightened. News travels fast on a campus, and the information of Don Crawford's tragic accident in the library had doubtless reached her during the day.

"Put her here," she said, indicating one of the two high cots.

The boys, relieved of their burden, made a hasty departure.

"I'll call Dr. Whitaker," Miss Johnson said after a brief examination of the wound. "And I'll get one of the other nurses to tend to Miss Chase."

We were left alone in the room only a moment or two when Miss Manning appeared, a brown-haired girl somewhat younger than Miss Johnson and very popular with her masculine patients. She removed the handkerchief bandage and washed the wound.

"I think you'd better go to the waiting room," she said to us. "I'll get Miss Chase into bed and ready for the doctor."

There seemed small danger of Miss Chase's conversational power returning for some time. So Carla and I withdrew immediately. No sooner were we alone than Carla turned to me.

"By the way," she said, "what was it you took out of Miss Chase's hand there in the library?"

"It was an envelope, an empty envelope, and if she mentions it try to find out what was in it, provided, of course, that they let you stay all night."

Now that we were actually within the walls of the infirmary, that possibility seemed very remote. The orderliness and discipline of the place were intimidating me. Nothing seems quite so impersonal as a hospital or a military camp. Rules and regulations preclude all exceptions to the usual routine. I felt that we would both be dismissed in short order after the arrival of Dr. Whitaker.

We had not long to wait for his appearance. Luckily he had been at home when Miss Johnson had telephoned. Within ten minutes he was at the hospital. After an examination he came into the waiting room. As always his manner was calm and slow, and his appearance as spruce as it had been at ten-thirty that morning.

"A bad concussion," he informed us. "Just how did it happen?"

I thought it best to repress some of the details. I told him what I had told the boys from the *Optima* offices, merely that the lights had gone out in the library and that Miss Chase had had a fall in the dark.

"Two accidents there within twenty-four hours," he mused gravely. "A strange coincidence."

"It seems strange to us, too," I conceded. "Miss Robinson would like to stay with her through the night if it can be managed."

I made the suggestion with some timidity, and I was glad of his hearty approval.

"A very good suggestion," he said. "In cases of this sort one can never tell when consciousness will return, or memory either. If Miss Robinson is a friend, it will seem natural to Miss Chase to have her there when the effects of the shock pass."

I forestalled Carla's denial of friendship with the remark, "That's just what we thought."

Dr. Whitaker looked at me rather keenly. "You know," he said, "it doesn't see altogether like the result of a fall. The wound looks more as if it had been caused by a blow. Perhaps Miss Chase herself can tell us more about it later."

"No doubt she can," I remarked briefly. "Well, I suppose there's nothing else I can do. I'll be around the first thing in the morning."

Dr. Whitaker and Carla were proceeding down the corridor when I took my departure. Over her shoulder Carla gave me a rather helpless look. I tried to smile reassuringly, but I was none too happy about the position in which I had left her.

What now? I thought to myself as I walked slowly along Maple Avenue. There was no longer any doubt whatsoever in my mind that there was something seriously amiss. The corridors and stacks of the library had taken on a sinister aspect that was much more than imaginary. The events of the evening had been real.

President Mittoff had not seemed much impressed by my remarks that morning. But what would he think now? I determined to stop at his house and acquaint him with the events of the evening. Strange things were transpiring, and I felt incapable of unraveling them by myself.

The president's house was wrapped in complete darkness as I approached it. I thumped the brass knocker on the door and heard the echoes reverberating down the long hallway. Only silence followed the echoes. No footsteps came down the stairway, and after a time I gave up my efforts and slowly retraced my footsteps down the walk. Perhaps President Mittoff was in his office, I thought. I turned back toward the campus. There was indeed a light in his office, but as I approached I saw that a trustee meeting was in progress. The room was gray with smoke and several men were seated around a long table. No use to linger there. Those meetings sometimes lasted interminably. Reluctantly I turned away.

Around a corner of the building I saw a light flash. Old Emil Schlachtman, the night watchman, turned his torch on me.

"Ach, it iss you, provessor. I t'ought it might be some of dos alumni up to der deviltry. Worse dan der boys dey are wit' der carryings-on."

We fell into step together.

"Sort of gloomy, isn't it, going around here night after night?" I asked him. "Don't you ever get a scare?"

"Vell, I don't know dat I do. You get kind of used to der dark. Id's vriendly," he replied philosophically.

"And then you have your dog," I answered as I saw the great creature bound shadow-like and silent ahead of us.

"Ya, Obie's a gut dog. I don't know vat I'll do wid him ven I leave. You, provessor, berhaps you'd like him?" His voice took on a pleading note.

I repressed a shudder. "No, I'm afraid I'm not a dog man," I told him. "But you aren't thinking of leaving, are you?"

"Vell, ya, I am t'inking of it." He hesitated a moment. "I vant to go back to der Vaterland to die. I got grandchildren I never seen. Ven I get der moneys saved up, den I go back and live in Heidelberg again. Ach, Heidelberg's der fine place. Der students ain't like dese boys, chust playing all der time."

He was, I saw, about to launch himself into an old man's reminiscences. But an idea struck me. I had no desire to listen to memories, at least none that went back farther than last night.

"By the way," I interrupted, "I was looking for you last night." A prevarication of twenty-four hours would not damn my soul, I hoped. And I had looked for him this evening. "I had an appointment to meet a friend, an alumnus, on the steps of the library at eight-thirty. But I missed him and I wondered if you had seen him around."

"Iss dot so?" he asked, turning slowly to peer at me. "I had ought to haf seen him. I was dere about eight-t'irty. Usually it iss exactly on der hour, but last night I vas late."

"And did you see any one around?" I persisted.

"Did I see any one? Der voods vas full of any ones. First I see a tall lady in vhite. I don't know who she vas. She chust disappear in der shrubbery. Pouf!" He blew a light breath into the air. "Den I see one of dos student desk clerks. She vent into der library."

"Miss Hubbard?" I suggested.

"Ya, Miss Hubbard. Dat's who it vas. Den I see Mr. Denman and Miss Robinson. Dey come out of der library in a big hurry."

His words opened new and unhappy channels in my thought. But I tried to keep my voice calm as I clung to my fabricated tale of hunting a friend. He was assuming body in my imagination.

"But that's all you saw? You didn't see a large man weighing about two hundred and twenty pounds? You couldn't very well miss him if he was about."

"No, I could not miss dat. I did not see any human elephants. Your friend vas not dere." I felt almost a smile in his voice, as if he saw through my inquiries.

"Then that's all right," I said. "He was probably detained, too. Thanks for the information. Goodnight. Here's where I turn."

"Auf wiederseh'n," he said to my vanishing back, and it *was* vanishing too. As fast as I could make it, I was hurrying to my room to jot down the names of the persons of whom he had spoken and the order of their appearance at the library.

CHAPTER IX

I DREW out a blank sheet of paper and spread it before me on my desk.

Thursday Evening, June 7th — 8:30, I headed it.

Characters in Order of Appearance

1. Tall lady in white; identity unknown. Disappears in shrubbery.
2. Agnes Hubbard. Enters library.
3. Miss Robinson and Mr. Denman. Hurry out of library.

I looked at this list and pondered. Certainly it was not long. But what it lost in length it made up in mystery. Who was the tall lady in white? She could have been any one of hundreds of persons. And why had she disappeared into the shrubbery? Was she meeting some one there? Was she merely hiding from Emil? Was she following some one? Was she looking for something in the shrubbery?

Each question led me down a blind alley. There was too little here to go on. I tried it from a new angle, putting myself in her place. Instantly an answer leaped to my mind. Windows! Often enough I myself had stepped into that shadowy foliage, and it had always been for one purpose — to obtain entrance to the library. I had harbored the nice conceit that the secret was mine alone. I saw now how ridiculous this idea had been. Any one might have chanced on those unlocked windows and might have been making use of them for as long as, or even longer, than I had.

I felt that I had taken a step, but only a short and very obvious one, in the right direction. Why had the unknown woman desired entrance into the building and who was she? The answers to these two questions might be perfectly innocent ones. But in the light of what had occurred in the stacks between eight and nine o'clock of that evening the presence of any one was, to say the least, questionable. The tall woman in white was an important factor. The question of her identity and of her purpose could not be disregarded. There was no possible identification in the fact that she had been dressed in white. I made a mental note to examine the shrubbery early the next morning.

I went on to my next notation: Agnes Hubbard. Enters library.

In itself the statement looked harmless. Agnes Hubbard went in and out of the library a dozen times a day. Ah! but there was the rub. Why should a girl who worked in the library during all her spare hours return there on an evening when the building was locked? There might be any number of reasonable answers. She might have had some unfinished piece of work to get out. But in any event why had she not mentioned to me her presence there at that hour? Her failure to do so gave a peculiar cast to the situation. Had she perhaps removed the envelope from its secret hiding place. Had she merely pretended to me that she didn't want to touch it again? Had she known all the time that it was gone? Did she know now what it contained?

My mind was buzzing with questions difficult to answer, but I pushed on to further suppositions. Had Agnes Hubbard seen something during that hour on Thursday evening — something that she wanted to hide? Had she known that Don Crawford was lying dead or unconscious in the stacks? And had she, herself, without request from Bertha Chase, gone to that fatal spot the following morning?

No, that was absurd. Her faint had been too real. Forewarned is forearmed. Had she known what lay in that spot she would have gone there, if at all, for only one purpose — to give the alarm. She would have cried out. But she would not have fainted. That was one theory I could discard. On Friday morning she had been innocent of all knowledge of Don's death, I felt sure. But that brought me back to the first question. What had she been doing in the library on Thursday evening? I would find that out the next morning. The girl was already frightened. I felt no compunction at the prospect of frightening her still further.

I looked at the last two names on the list, and a blankness of doubt and bewilderment settled over

me. Carla Robinson and Mark Denman. I did not
like to see even their names coupled together there
in my handwriting. And they had been actually together at eight-thirty Thursday evening. Together
and hurrying from the library. My head swam diz-
zily. I had never admired Mark Denman. Now I
hated him. But I had to admit that he had a way
with the ladies. Too much of a way to suit me. He
was surrounded by girls in the library. Surely Carla
had seen that. But to be singled out by him might
seem an honor. I had small knowledge of the feminine heart, but from all my reading I had deduced
that it was an inexplicable organ. Had Carla been
flattered? I could not let my mind dwell on the
point.

Had they together made the gruesome discovery?
Were they in any way implicated, either together or
individually? Was Mark Denman the guilty person,
and had he hurried Carla away from a discovery she
had been about to make? Was her display of amazement at my suspicions a piece of good acting? What
did she know or guess?

Up and down, around and over, my mind circled
like a mad Ferris wheel getting nowhere. Must I suspect Carla too? My heart shrank from it even as my
mind told me that I could exempt no one. All I
knew now was that she had been with Mark Denman at eight-thirty Thursday evening and that they
had been hurrying. Why did people hurry? To get
some place. To get away from some place. I could
go no further. My mind, baffled and hurt, repeated

only one thing — she had not told me, she had not told me. Well, why should she? I demanded. But that let in such a confusion of remarkable emotions that I reached in my pocket for a cigarette.

My hand encountered a crumpled piece of paper. I had forgotten the manila envelope. I drew it out now and smoothed out its creases. Rumpled as it was, it had its story to tell. Bertha Chase had clenched it in her hand there in the alcove and I had not improved its appearance by jamming it into my pocket. But when these resultant creases were smoothed out, there remained four strong outlines that would not be eradicated. They marked clearly the original contents of the envelope. And I knew that those contents had been a bulky pamphlet of some sort.

My involuntary sigh of relief was audible to my own ears. I knew that Agnes Hubbard had not told me her complete story, but at least this envelope substantiated part of what she had said. I need not wholly distrust her.

And if these four people had all been in, out, and around the library at precisely eight-thirty there was no telling how many others had been there before or after that hour. Perhaps I need distrust none of the four persons listed on the paper before me. It was with a feeling of relief that I got into bed, where I tossed restlessly all night long and dreamed over and over of skulking through the library after Carla Robinson and Mark Denman who turned into volumes of "The Golden Bough" and slid through the shelves before me.

The early sunlight pouring into my bedroom roused me from this troubled sleep. Further rest was impossible. Already the air was hot and heavy with promise of one of those sultry days which the middle west brews to such perfection. Again I tiptoed about my room, getting into my clothes as quietly as possible. Again the cardinal's song greeted me, but today the notes filled me with the poignancy of anxiety rather than of ecstasy.

Again I breakfasted at one of the white topped tables of George and Harry's, and I thought of my exuberance of only twenty-four hours earlier. Then I had been happy at the thought of the summer days I should spend with Carla Robinson exploring the loveliness of this little college town. But now I was reminded that Mark Denman also would be on hand to share the hours of her companionship, and I wondered if Carla had been as quick to inform him of her summer appointment as she had been to tell me about it.

It was only eight o'clock when I walked down University Avenue to Maple Street and toward the infirmary. A few sleepy Seniors were lounging about the fraternity houses in pajamas and bathrobes, sentimentalizing over their departure probably, and making plans for this day of festivity which was given over to their affairs and which would terminate in a banquet which the authorities hoped would be sufficiently staid to uphold the good name of Kingsley.

The door of the hospital was open to what breeze

there was, and I found Miss Johnson at her desk in the main hall.

"She was just the same all night," she told me in answer to my inquiry. "But Miss Manning thinks there's a slight change now. I've just sent for Dr. Whitaker. If you'd like to stay you can sit in the waiting room."

I was there perhaps an hour, during which time I saw the doctor enter and, after a few words with Miss Johnson, move off toward the room where Bertha Chase had been installed. As I sat there, my thoughts began again their endless queries about Carla. What had she been doing in the library Thursday evening? If she knew anything about what had taken place there between eight and nine o'clock, I had certainly been most unwise in urging her to spend the past night here in the infirmary. She had been reluctant to do so, I knew, and perhaps she had reasons of which I was ignorant.

I was conscious suddenly that there was some commotion in the corridors. Miss Manning came running along the hall. She returned in a moment with another nurse. Between them they wheeled a large contrivance which I later learned was an air cooler. There was the sound of a voice talking on and on. I could not catch the words, but from the inflection I could tell that something was being repeated over and over in despairing tones.

Suddenly there was a loud, shrill cry. Then quite distinctly I heard the words, "You, you, oh go away, go away, go away. I hate you. I hate you."

Then Carla came running along the hall, and I forgot all my troubled dreams of the past night as I saw her standing in the doorway with flushed cheeks and tearful eyes. For a moment or two she could not speak. I led her to a divan and she sat there trembling. One hand held my arm tightly as a child's might have. Finally she spoke.

"Oh, it was awful," she said. "All night she didn't move. Miss Manning sat beside her, and I tried to rest on the other cot. Then this morning she began to moan and to move a little. They sent for Dr. Whitaker, and after he came she started to talk. She kept her eyes closed all the time. I didn't need your notebook. She just said the same thing over and over, 'It wasn't my letter. It was just a toy. It wasn't my letter. It was just a toy.'"

I felt my scalp creep. "A toy?" I asked. "Did she always use that word 'toy'?"

"No, she changed it once or twice. 'Just something for a child,' she said. And then she would laugh, so softly and so hopelessly. Dr. Whitaker whispered to me to talk to her, so I did."

"What did you say?" I questioned eagerly.

"I said, 'Never mind. It's all right.' But she kept moaning and saying, 'I thought it was my letter. That's why I took it.' She seemed so worried. I wanted to calm her, so I said the first thing I thought of. I thought it would quiet her. I said, 'I'll get your letter for you.' And then" Carla's voice broke, but she went on, "and then she opened her eyes and looked right at me. She screamed and pointed at me, and her eyes were terrible. 'You, you,' she cried, 'oh go away, go away, go away. I hate you. I hate you.' I was so frightened I ran right out of the room."

There were dark circles under Carla's eyes and her hair lay in damp, dark curls about her forehead. Her hand still clung to my arm. I smoothed it gently. She didn't even notice. But her breathing grew more regular. She smiled rather ironically. "I wasn't much of a success, was I?"

Dr. Whitaker came in then, his face graver than ever. "There's nothing you two can do here," he said. "Miss Chase is unconscious." And at Carla's exclamation of dismay, "You're not to blame, my dear. She's had a shock. Nature must take care of her. We can only wait. Probably she didn't even recognize you. You were just some part of a dark dream she'd been having."

Carla smiled faintly in gratitude for his kindness, but I could see that she was not convinced.

"But how long will she be like this?" I asked

"No one can say. It may be hours or days. Concussion does strange things to the mind and the body."

Carla left us to comb her hair and freshen up, and Dr. Whitaker turned to me, his fingers playing slowly with his lower lip.

"It looks a bit queer to me, Allen," he said. "Two accidents in the library within so few hours." His keen eyes looked into mine. "There's something strange going on, I'm thinking."

"I agree with you, sir. And Don Crawford was my

friend. I'm determined to ferret it out. I have the president's authority," I added a bit pompously.

"Good for you. I don't like the looks of things. If I can help, let me know."

"You can do this," I said. "Have Miss Manning jot down anything Miss Chase says. Whether it sounds sane or not. I think you'll find a notebook and pencil in the room."

Dr. Whitaker raised his eyebrows. "So that's how it was," he remarked. "Miss Robinson was staying so you wouldn't miss anything."

I felt rather ill at ease. But he laid his hand on my arm. "And quite right, too. Quite right. It's best to leave no stone unturned. But no more questions, mind you."

When Carla returned he looked at her white face. "You'd better get some sleep now, my child. I'll notify you if there's any change." He turned down the corridor as I held the screen open for Carla.

But it wasn't sleep that Carla needed first. It was breakfast. We stopped in at a nearby tea room, and as she sipped her coffee I watched some of the tiredness leave her face. I longed to ask her some of the questions that had been troubling me for the past ten hours, but I was restrained by the look of weariness in her face. Would she think it mere jealous curiosity if I asked why she and Mark Denman had been together in the library Thursday evening? Perhaps it would be better for her to think that than realize that on my list of suspects her name, too, now had a place. I should have to question her sooner or later

I knew, but just then I preferred that it should be later.

"I'm afraid I've messed things up terribly," Carla said finally as we sat pulling at our cigarettes and looking at each other. "I didn't get any information for you, and I certainly didn't do Miss Chase any good. She might have been all right if I hadn't spoken to her."

"You did just what I would have done myself," I told her. "No one could tell the effect it would have, and Dr. Whitaker suggested that you speak to her. After you've had a nap I'd like to see you again, if I may."

"You're going to Don Crawford's funeral, aren't you?" she asked. "I'd like to go too if you'll stop for me."

We parted with that understanding, and I determined that before the day was over I would ask her the questions that disturbed me. As it happened I was spared the necessity of inquiring, but at the moment I could not foresee the events that would bring unasked the information I sought.

My mind was, if possible, now more confused than ever. Jealousy and doubt fought with an emotion that was new and amazingly powerful. I was, I could see, in danger of making an abject fool of myself. All the time I had sat with Carla while her tired eyes smiled at me across her breakfast, two lines of Irish poetry had whirled through my mind:

"Put your head, darling, darling, darling,
   Your darling black head my heart above — "

For all I knew Mark Denman might be a murderer and Carla might be in love with him, or she might even be a murderer herself, but that was the ridiculous, poetic way I felt about her.

My first task was now to comb the shrubbery about the library in search of a clue to the mysterious lady in white of whom Emil had told me. But look as I did for an hour I could find no identifying trace. There were footprints galore, so many that they obliterated my own, but no more envelopes or gold links repaid my searching. Considering the fact that I had made small use of what clues I had, I was just as well pleased to find no further items to puzzle me. As far as I could see, I had so far arrived exactly nowhere. I was wandering in a fog of supposition and suspicion, and the one person whose actions seemed most suggestive and mysterious lay unconscious in the college hospital.

I thought back over the events of the previous evening. What had Bertha Chase been doing at Agnes Hubbard's desk in the alcove? Obviously she had not just found the manila envelope which I later took from her clenched hand. The thoroughness with which Agnes Hubbard and I had searched the desk assured me that the letter had been previously removed. Bertha Chase must then have been returning it. And to return it meant that she had obtained it at some earlier time — some time after Don Crawford had placed it in the secret opening. Had she witnessed its hiding? But if she had taken it, why return it?

Suddenly a great cloud of fog blew away from my brain. Bertha Chase had been hovering around that morning when I entered the library for my appointed meeting with Agnes Hubbard. She had heard me say I was going to look up a book in the stacks. In all probability she had seen Agnes Hubbard follow me a few moments later. I recalled Agnes Hubbard's words as we talked together in the basement stacks. I had thought her only nervous when she whispered, "Listen! Did you hear something just then?" But what if there had been some one there outside in the shrubbery? And what if that person had been Bertha Chase? It would have been difficult to hear all we said, but she might easily have understood enough to tell her the hiding place of the manila envelope. And it was a manila envelope she was seeking, an envelope that contained a letter in her handwriting that was a confession of her secret marriage.

I pictured her suddenly slipping from her hiding place, hurrying into the side entrance, opening Agnes Hubbard's desk, taking the envelope and concealing it in her dress. It would have taken only a minute or two. She would have been safely away while we were coming upstairs. And all the time we were in the basement, Don Crawford's treasure, whatever it was, had been safe in Agnes Hubbard's desk. I felt sure my conjecture was the correct one. The envelope had been removed only a moment or two before we began our search for it.

But what had happened later?

My mind clicked the answer to me as surely as if

it had been a witness in the box and the rest of me the
prosecuting attorney. Then, later, when she got to
her room perhaps, she had opened the envelope and
had found, not her letter, but — what was it she had
cried in the infirmary when she was regaining consciousness? — "It wasn't my letter. It was just a toy.
Just something for a child." But if it had been only
a toy, only something for a child, why had Don Crawford ever thought it valuable? At that question the
fog swept in again over my mind. I could push my
inquiries no further. But I felt that I had made some
progress, vague as it was.

In the sane light of day my notion of again carrying my suspicions to President Mittoff weakened
considerably. It was all too tenuous as yet. I could
imagine his amused smile if I should tell him of Bertha Chase's meaningless words. "A toy?" he would
probably say. "The whole thing seems rather like
child's play to me." Then he would go on to talk
of unpleasant publicity and I should be left exactly
where I was now, only I would be robbed of another
degree or so of dignity. He had told me to investigate
the matter myself. Very well, I would do so. And I
would begin with Agnes Hubbard.

As I walked slowly into the library I thought how
much easier investigations are in theory than in ac-
tuality, investigations of a crime at any rate. And
especially when one is not clothed with legal authority. For no matter how much support President Mittoff gave me, no matter how much authority he be-
stowed upon me, my inquiries had nothing of the third

degree about them. No one would feel the slightest necessity of answering questions just because I asked them. On the other hand this very circumstance carried with it an advantage. The fact that I was unofficial might induce people to talk more freely than they would to a detective who was a complete stranger, particularly if they felt inclined to talk about other people. Idealistic as a college community seems to outsiders, gossip is not unknown within the sacred precincts. Tact and sympathy were what I needed for my undertaking. I buckled them on and proceeded toward Agnes Hubbard's desk.

CHAPTER X

Agnes HUBBARD was tidying up the filing desk in preparation for her noon hour off, and the idea came to me that our talk might prove more efficacious over a luncheon table than in this region of musty tomes. There is something solemn about a library, something stern and even a little grim. I felt that to loosen her tongue Agnes Hubbard needed an environment with a more ephemeral suggestion. And what, I thought to myself, is so ephemeral as vanishing food? So with a guileful smile on my lips which made me feel like the wolf in "Little Red Riding Hood" I suggested that we lunch together at the Tulip Tree Inn about ten miles out from town.

Agnes Hubbard cast what seemed to me an involuntary glance up toward the balcony. Then in an almost defiant manner she replied, "Yes, I'd like to go."

There was something back of that glance and that manner, I thought, as I ran across to Miss MacIntyre's to get my car. Or had I become so suspicious that I read into every expression some suppressed feeling? Then I remembered the *Optima* offices and Benjamin Morris. He and Agnes Hubbard had been together at the presentation of "Peer Gynt." Perhaps there was a romance there, and, being a Senior, Benjamin Morris had gone off with his brethren for the day, leaving a slightly miffed Junior at the filing desk.

My roadster, christened "School's Out" in a carefree moment, had not been out of the garage for three days, but true to the much advertised boast of its maker, it responded instantly to my touch. Agnes Hubbard was waiting on the library steps. Her cheeks were flushed, and the green dress she wore gave to her always interesting eyes the shifting colors of deep sea water. There was an enigmatic quality about the girl that set her apart from the ordinary college student. It would be difficult to predict this girl's future. She smiled charmingly as she got into the car. Soon we were leaving a cloud of dust behind us.

The Tulip Tree Inn was crowded as it always is, but we were fortunate in procuring a table removed from the others and close to the edge of the brook that tumbled past over a rocky bed. Not wishing to ruin the girl's meal I did not introduce the topic trembling on the tip of my tongue until the ices were served.

Then I decided to adopt bold tactics.

I leaned toward her confidentially. "Miss Hubbard," I began, "you were right the other day when you accused me of thinking Don Crawford's death was perhaps not accidental."

Her eyes widened, and a look — was it of fright? —

flickered over them. The spoon in her red-tipped fingers trembled ever so slightly.

"I think it is about time that we stop sparring. You suspected also that he had met with foul play, didn't you?"

She was looking down now at her glass of orange ice. "Why, no," she said slowly. "Not really. I was just excited."

She spoke the words carefully. It was plain that she was on her guard. Why? I wondered.

Guileful again, I had recourse to flattery. I told her how anxious I was, hinting suggestively at certain discoveries I had made. "You have been of inestimable value, so far," I said. "And there are one or two other little things you might help me with. You were in the library Thursday evening, weren't you?"

I watched the color fade from her face, and I reminded myself that fainting was not impossible to her. But even as her lips took on a bluish hue, some inner strength, that I had admired before in the girl, seemed to assert itself. She drew a deep breath and lifted her head a bit higher.

"Yes, I was," she said. "Did you think I would deny it?"

I was almost angry. "No, of course I didn't expect you to deny it. I only wished you'd told me so of your own accord."

"There was nothing to tell. I saw nothing."

But I could see by her stiff, frozen-looking lips that though there might be nothing to tell, there was at any rate something to hide, and I was determined to discover what it was.

"How long were you there?" I persisted.

"About ten minutes. I went at eight-thirty to get a book I was reading. I suppose what you're thinking is that I knew what was in that envelope and stole it myself from my own desk and then murdered Don Crawford so he wouldn't find out."

"Don't be silly," I replied, but I had to admit to myself that it could have been possible. Certainly not probable, however.

"Did you see any one in the library while you were there?"

"Why, yes, I saw two people. I saw Mr. Denman and Miss Robinson."

"And where were they?" I asked, trying to keep my voice normal.

"In Miss Robinson's office." She caught her breath.

I hazarded a guess. "I suppose you saw them when you were looking for Benjamin Morris."

All her feeble defenses crumbled. "How did you know?" she asked, and I recalled it was this question that characters in fiction often ask of the most astute detective. Immediately I felt that I was getting on.

"Oh, I have ways." I answered with what I hoped was a Muradic nonchalance though my smoking is confined to Spuds. "But you didn't find him, did you?"

"No," she replied flatly. "You know I didn't."

Of course I knew nothing of the sort, but as long as she thought I did, so much the better.

"You didn't think to look in the stacks, I suppose?"

As soon as I had asked the question I saw that I had touched her on the raw. She drew back almost wincing. I had found out something. That was exactly where she feared Benjamin Morris had been. But why? As she continued to stare at me in wordless fright, I decided quickly to appear to interpret that fear as indignation.

"Forgive me," I said. "That was an unspeakable suggestion. My mind is in such a whirl I don't know what I'm saying half the time."

She drew a quick breath of relief, and as we lingered listening to the water gurgle over the rocks I turned the conversation to other channels. By diverting her attention I hoped later to catch her off her guard.

So, afterwards, as we drove back to town, I brought up the subject again. "Forgive me for having a one-track mind," I began, "but I can't keep my thoughts off the matter. You knew, didn't you, when you saw that arm dangling through the shelf, that it was Don Crawford's?"

I glanced at her quickly. Her eyes looked straight ahead. She said nothing.

"The ring was unmistakable," I continued. "I knew it at once."

I did not realize what a lucky shot I had made until I heard her catch her breath. "Yes, I knew," she said with something like a sob in voice, "and I suppose you know all about that ring. I suppose he told you I'd given it back to him just two weeks ago."

I did some quick thinking. What was it Bertha Chase had said in her letter? Something about knowing all about his present love affair. So Agnes Hubbard had been the girl.

It is of tremendous advantage at times to have half your attention elsewhere. I expended my complete amazement at this revelation by successfully manipulating the car around a large beer truck. That accomplished I was ready with my reply. It seemed a safe one. "What made you change your mind?"

"I never felt quite sure," she confided, and something in the tone of her voice told me that she was relieved to be talking about it. "I was flattered at first at being the only one of hundreds of students to have attracted his attention. And I was surprised. He'd always seemed so quiet. I never dreamed he could care so much for any one. So, though I didn't promise to marry him, I did say I'd consider it. That was in April. He wanted me to wear his ring, not as an engagement ring, but just as a sort of a link between us."

I started at the word "link", thinking of the unmatched gold ones locked in my desk drawer. But I could scarcely believe that it was Don Crawford she was talking about. That quiet hermit married to one girl and making love to another! It was incomprehensible.

"I did like him," Agnes Hubbard continued. "I liked him awfully and I feel — oh, I can't tell you how, now that he's dead. I had his ring for a while. I wore it on a chain around my neck, under my dress, you know."

"On a gold chain?" The question shot from me before I thought.

"Yes," she answered quietly, "this one." She touched the chain at her neck from which now hung an old-fashioned locket. But one glance at it assured me of its innocence. The links of this chain were traced with a delicate filigree. The two sets of links I had discovered were both plain.

"But later on," she continued, "I found I didn't love him — not enough anyway. Not so much — " She hesitated and concluded lamely, "not so much as I thought I ought to, to marry him. And now that he's dead I feel terribly. But I couldn't have done anything else."

"Of course not."

Poor girl, I thought, reproaching herself for having hurt a man already married. I tried to picture Don Crawford as the rascal which my discoveries told me he was. It was impossible. Slow, quiet Don caught in the net of a secret marriage, involved in a love affair with a student. It didn't fit somehow. How he must have suffered, entangled by Bertha Chase, for I saw her always as the pursuer, and in love with Agnes Hubbard.

And now here she was beside me telling so much more by her hesitancy than by her words. Telling by her silence, by her anxiety, that it was Benjamin Morris whom she loved, that it was her love for him that had caused the return of Don Crawford's ring. Looking at me back there by the brook with fear in her eyes, a fear that Benjamin Morris had been in the stacks that night, had had a hand in that dark business which was called an accident but which she too thought was a murder. I recalled how inadvertently, how immediately she had let that thought slip into words yesterday morning. Jealousy is a potent force. Perhaps all the more dangerous in youth when years have not yet fashioned experience and philosophy into a pair of crutches. She had no doubt told Benjamin Morris all about her harmless affair with Don Crawford. And out of all proportion to the facts he had been insanely jealous. So jealous that now she feared the consequences.

"You are not to blame," I told her. "Who of us can tell why it is that love comes and goes?" I thought of Carla as I uttered the platitude, and it seemed to me that I was speaking of ancient profundities never voiced till now.

"You will find love someday," I prophesied, and watching the flush creep up her neck and over her face I felt like a cad. Yes, it was Benjamin Morris, I felt sure. And had he really been in the stacks Thursday evening as she feared?

I slowed "School's Out" down to twenty miles. "I should like to see you in love," I mused in fatherly tones. "There is something so essentially truthful in your nature that you would make of the experience a beautiful thing. But just now I wish more than anything that you had gone into the stacks Thursday evening."

She was silent a long time as we idled along. But her hands were busy. What was it she was doing? Ah! then I saw. Slowly and carefully she was digging at that red enamel on her nails, pulling it off bit by bit. What did it signify? Was she discarding in her thoughts some artificial and concealing defense?

Then she spoke, her tone low, almost inaudible, so that I had to bend my head to hear her.

"I almost did go there," she confessed. "I stood right by the door ready to go in, but I heard a noise and it frightened me. It was all dark and the noise came suddenly."

I held my breath, afraid to interrupt her lest her mood change suddenly. She spoke as if she were almost unconscious of my presence.

"It was a loud bang, like a heavy stick falling on the floor. It frightened me, and I didn't go in. I just stood there a minute. Then I almost ran out of the building."

"And that's all?" I asked.

"That's all," she said, and now her eyes stared almost wildly at me. "I don't know why I told you. I wish I hadn't."

I longed to offer her some word of assurance or comfort. But there was nothing I could say. She must not know that I guessed her secret, that she had shown me all too clearly her love for Benjamin Morris and her fear for him.

"You have been very good," I said as I let her out at the library drive. "And you must not blame yourself because you were unable to return Don Crawford's regard. Some day you will make some other man very happy."

But I saw immediately that I had said the wrong thing. Her eyes filled with tears, and I knew that she was thinking that already she might have betrayed some one for whom she cared.

CHAPTER XI

I HAD time for a shower, a change, and some reflection before I mounted the steps of 711 Campus Avenue where Carla roomed in the house of a Mrs. Titcomb, the widow of a former professor. The gentle old lady herself opened the door at my ring, and I waited a moment or two in the cool, high-ceilinged living room before Carla came down. Her cheeks were flushed, her eyes bright, although she could not repress a yawn as she entered the room.

"I just woke up half an hour ago," she said. "Sleeping in the daytime is terrible in hot weather. I feel as if I'd never be cool again."

"You're good to go with me," I said. "There won't be many there."

In point of fact there were only eight there, including ourselves and the Methodist minister, Dr. Tressel. Mark Denman, Agnes Hubbard, and three professors, Mr. Straight of the Physics department, Mr. Kelton and Mr. Hatton, both of the Chemistry department, were the only others. The latter three had taken their lunches and dinners at the same boarding house where Don and I had also eaten until it closed the week before commencement. I had thought that perhaps Dr. Tyndale and Miss Mac-Intyre would be present, although they had no reason other than sympathy to bring them to the service, and I had to admit that the hot weather put something of a strain on a quality that was at best not compelling.

It seemed strange to think that Bertha Chase lay unconscious at the college hospital as these last words were spoken over Don. I could not bring myself even to think of her as Mrs. Crawford, though I supposed that as soon as she had recovered she would make public her marriage and would claim what few possessions and funds Don had left.

The service was very short. In view of what I had learned from Agnes Hubbard that noon, I had anticipated it as something of an ordeal. My mind was in turmoil. If all that I had learned was true, Don Crawford was assuredly not the person I had thought him. But looking at his still face with its high forehead and fine nose, with its expression of calm and dignity, all my old regard for the man came flooding back. I was not in possession of all the facts. There were extenuating circumstances, I felt sure, that would excuse the apparent ugliness of the situation. The key to it all lay with Bertha Chase, lying as motionless as the figure in the coffin before us. And there was no knowing when she would be able to talk.

I almost wished, as we stood about the open grave

in the cemetery, that it was Bertha Chase who was being lowered into the earth and that it was Don who lay in the hospital with an even chance for recovery. But every one is entitled to his own destiny. Bitter as I might feel toward her, there was no changing the mysterious workings of Fate.

It was when we were leaving the grave that a thing happened which seemed like an omen of success and which sent my heart, even at that sad hour, bounding to the skies. Mark Denman moved over to walk back to the driveway with Carla, and I heard him say, "Will you have dinner with me to-night at the Tavern?" And Carla, raising her voice a trifle, replied, "Thank you. I'm dining with Mr. Allen this evening."

I opened the door of the roadster, smiling broadly.

"Then you don't mind?" she asked.

"Mind! I don't even say, 'I wish I'd thought of it first', for I have thought of it every minute of the day, but I wasn't sure you'd forgiven me yet for making you go through those hours at the hospital."

"You know I don't blame you." Her voice was gentle. "I blame only myself for bungling things."

Opportunity knocks but once, I thought and plunged boldly in. "Well, I'll take you to dinner on one condition only. There's something more I want you to do for me."

"Do you want me to spend another night in the hospital?" Her voice sounded a little uncontrolled.

"No, nothing as bad as that. I want to look over

some things in Miss Chase's room, and I hoped you would accompany me. It would lend more credence to the story I'm going to tell her landlady if I were accompanied by a woman."

She hesitated a moment. "All these things seem so underhanded," she said. "But I suppose they're necessary. All right, I'll go with you."

"It will be quite easy," I assured her. "I lived for four years in that house. Miss Leighton, who owns it, used to have only men roomers though this year it's been given over to the feminine contingent. When the Men's Faculty Club opened this year, most of her roomers went there."

"Why didn't you?" Carla inquired.

"Oh, I didn't want so much sociability. Miss MacIntyre and Dr. Tyndale suit me better. They never notice my comings and goings. I've been especially glad of that lately."

"Have you?" she said, apparently not appreciating that the significance of my remark was that most of my comings and goings during the past months had been motivated by her presence at Kingsley. A little worried frown furrowed her forehead.

Across the front of Miss Leighton's yellow frame house extended a wide porch. The house looked ordinary enough from the street, but it trailed backward to a prodigious depth. It had been built in the era of twelve-children families, but of late years it had been used to house lonely bachelors or spinsters. It was sad to consider that those rooms, which had echoed with the cries and laughter of so many childish sorrows and joys, had grown silent to the need of adult heads bent over books and papers.

Miss Leighton herself was one of those robust souls who, without much education themselves, find joy in the knowledge that they are contributing, somewhat vicariously, to the education of the world. When her house had sheltered ten or twelve bachelors she had taken great pride in her "professors", feeling herself a peer among the other landladies of the town.

She greeted me now with loud exclamations of joy, acknowledging my introduction of Carla by a hearty handshake and by a keen scrutiny that showed me that she was sizing her up as a possible roomer.

"Land sakes, Mr. Allen," she said loudly, "if I'd of known you was coming I'd of freshened up a bit. These last days I have my hands full, I can tell you, and I declare I haven't sat down all day."

"We've only stopped in for a minute, Miss Leighton. We have an errand to do for Miss Chase."

"Oh, the poor lamb." Miss Leighton was a perfect jelly of sympathy. "How is she now? I just heard this morning she was in the hospital."

"She's a little better," I hastened to say, lest Carla betray the real state of affairs. There are several things she'd like, and if you don't mind we'll just go up to her room and bundle them up for her."

I had expected some remonstrance against my hunting through a young lady's belongings, and I had determined to be firm.

She did indeed begin the attack immediately. "Now

you just sit right here and rest. I'll help Miss Robinson." She was already on her feet. But I was spared the test of wills, for at that opportune moment the doorbell rang. "Oh, that's Miss Freeman come to see me about the church supper. I'm afraid you'll have to excuse me after all. Go right on up. It's the second door to the left."

We lost no time in getting up the stairs. The room looked decidedly disordered. Clothing was tossed over chairs and bed, two of the dresser drawers were partly open, and the desk was littered with papers.

"I'll take the desk, if you'll go through the dresser," I said.

"But what am I to look for?"

"Anything resembling a small gold chain, particularly if it's broken. And you might bundle together some night clothes while you're about it. We've got to offer some evidence to Miss Leighton, and we can leave them at the hospital. Miss Chase really may need them later on."

With as much speed as possible I attacked the muddle on the desk. I hardly knew what I was looking for, but I thought there might be some note in Don Crawford's handwriting or a marriage license perhaps. I found that the task was less arduous than I had first thought it. Although the letters and papers were in confusion there were not many of them, and to my searching they disclosed nothing unusual. There were some cancelled checks which I glanced through but found unimportant. There were unanswered letters from friends and relatives, university bulletins and some bills. But as I delved deeper into the jumble I came upon something that held my immediate attention. It was a crumpled manila envelope which had once been sealed but which bore no address or other writing. It lay in a ball in the right-hand corner of the desk. I smoothed it out and drew forth its contents. Written in a fine, compact hand that I knew well it read:

"MY DEAR MR. DENMAN:

Thank you very much for asking me to attend the commencement concert with you this evening, but I have so much work to do that I am unable to accept your invitation.

Sincerely,

CARLA ROBINSON."

Behind me I heard a low exclamation. With wide eyes Carla was looking over my shoulder.

"Why, what does it mean?" she asked. "How did it get here?"

"I haven't the faintest idea," I answered, stuffing it into my pocket, which seemed to have become a constant repository for manila envelopes. "We'll have to determine that later. Have you found anything?" I saw that she held some object enclosed in her hand.

"Nothing but this," she answered, laying before me an old-fashioned gold bracelet. It was the kind that has, in addition to its clasp, the safeguard of a small chain. As I looked at the bracelet lying before me, I saw that the chain was formed of small gold links. But they were not continuous. In the exact middle the chain had been snapped in two. It was the sort of thing I had been hoping to find, but now that it lay before me I was almost speechless.

"Good work, Carla," I said, slipping it into my pocket. "Now let's get out of here. Miss Freeman may not stay forever."

But she was still there, talking animatedly of chicken pie and scalloped potatoes as we descended the stairs.

"Thanks very much, Miss Leighton," I called as I went through the hall.

"Give my love to poor Miss Chase," she replied.

"She'll need somebody's love a lot," I mumured to Carla, stepping rather viciously on the starter of the innocuous "School's Out."

"What do you mean? What are you thinking?"

"I hardly know myself. But first we're going to have a talk." I drove rapidly through the village and out onto a little-frequented road. "You'll have to help me clear up a point or two before I know just where we are," I said stopping under a shady locust tree. "Have you any idea how that note of yours could possibly have come into the possession of Miss Chase?"

"No, not the remotest, but I think now that Mr. Denman must have been telling the truth when he said he'd never received it."

"Suppose you begin at the beginning. I'm rather at sea."

"Well, I'll tell you everything I know, but it's not very pleasant."

I had always noticed that Carla blushed very easily, and I felt now that the flush on her cheeks was not wholly the result of the sultriness of the day.

She looked down as she spoke. "When I came to my office Thursday morning there was a note under my door. It was from Mr. Denman saying that he had two tickets for the concert that evening and that he hoped I would accompany him. That's the way he does things." She paused.

"And why didn't you want to?" I asked, my voice foolish with hope. "Were you really so busy?"

"No, of course not. I could have gone if I'd wanted to. But I don't like him."

"Has he been bothering you?" Inwardly I was cursing my vocal chords, for the sounds I was making sounded like the heroic tones of a hero in a cheap melodrama.

"Yes, a little," she answered. "But you don't need to kill him for it."

I did not at the time appreciate the trenchancy of this remark, but I was to remember it a few minutes later.

"And so you wrote a note of regret," I said, prodding her memory. "What did you do with it?"

"I was rather silly about it perhaps, but I didn't want to argue the matter with him. I couldn't just hand him the note. I might as well have told him in words as to do that. But toward noon I saw Don Crawford going over some catalogues in the stacks. I asked him to give it to Mr. Denman. And that's the last I know of it."

"But you said something about Denman's not having received it."

"Oh, yes. Well, to make my story good I went back to the office in the evening. I was a little afraid he'd disregard my note and call at the house for me anyway. And that's what he did, but when Mrs. Titcomb told him I wasn't there he came over to the library and up to my office. That's when he said he'd never received the note. I didn't believe him. It was rather unpleasant." She stopped for a moment. "I found I couldn't get rid of him. So rather than stay there I went to the concert after all."

"And you didn't see any one else in the library?"

"No, I was too angry to notice, I suppose; though I did think once that I heard footsteps on the balcony. By the way, what were you doing yourself that evening?"

I stared at her in amazement. It had never occurred to me that any one would check up on my own activities.

"You haven't a monopoly on catechism, have you?" she asked soberly.

"No, of course I haven't. As a matter of fact I was taking a walk in the country."

At my reply she began suddenly and gently to weep. The full significance of her tears and of her previous remark swept over me. She thought I had murdered Don Crawford! But the thought caused her tears. She cared enough to cry.

"Carla," I said, "Carla, darling, don't cry, please. If you only knew the things I've been thinking. I knew, you see, that you were in the library with Denman that evening."

She drew farther into her corner. "Did you see me?" she asked. "Was it you on the balcony?"

"Certainly it wasn't," I said emphatically, inwardly cursing myself for a fool. "The night watchman told me. He saw you both coming out."

Suddenly she began to laugh. "And you thought I had committed the murder."

"No matter what I've thought I've always adored you," I said impetuously.

Oh, gone on the fragrance of the locust blossoms was all my discretion, all my reticence. I, who was trying to rival Sherlock Holmes, was sitting on a quiet roadside making love to a girl who might still have difficulty in convincing a jury of her own innocence.

I looked helplessly at Carla. I had not thought her cheeks could grow redder, but they had. I seized her hands. "Later — later there is something else I want to tell you."

Her eyes were beautiful, full of a soft light, and she had not withdrawn her hands. I bent my head and kissed them.

We were silent on the return drive. There was a golden light over the hills, and I thought that once or twice Carla looked at her hands rather musingly.

CHAPTER XII

BACK in my room I went immediately to my desk where I had locked away the two sets of gold links I had picked up in the stacks the preceding morning. I compared them carefully with the chain of the bracelet. What with one thing and another my hands were shaking so that I could scarcely handle the fragile objects. And my excitement did not lessen when I discovered that one pair of links was identical with the chain. Looking at them through a reading glass, I could see where they had been jerked out of their position. The two links that I had found were intact, but those at the broken ends of the chain had sprung open. I recalled the spot where I had found them, near the table about eight feet from Don Crawford's body, and I remembered Bertha Chase's dropped handkerchief and the sweeping movement she had made in picking it up. She knew then where it had broken. It was evidence, and she did not want it discovered.

The case against her looked black indeed. There was her letter that I had found in Don Crawford's pocket, a letter with a threat in it. And the time limit of the threat was the very evening on which Don had met his death. I tried to visualize the scene. Just how the killing had been accomplished I could not determine, but I could see quite clearly Bertha Chase bending over the inert form, abstracting a manila envelope which in the excitement and possible panic of the moment she had thought to be her own guilty confession.

There was no question in my mind that the envelope she had obtained was the one we had just found in her room — Carla's note to Mr. Denman. No doubt Don had forgotten all about it. Carla had given it to him shortly before noon, she said. It had been at noon, as we crossed the campus together, that Don had confided to me his discovery of something valuable. Whatever that find had been, it had quite evidently put all other matters out of his mind.

As I went on to a further consideration of Bertha Chase's activities, I began to pace the floor. In her haste she had extracted the wrong envelope without taking time at that moment to examine the contents. She had carried it home only to discover her error; then afraid, perhaps, of that dead body, she had hesitated to return to the library that night. Instead she had waited until the next morning, when she had sent Agnes Hubbard for a book, located, as she well knew, near the spot where the body lay. Ah! that had been her mistake. She had not counted on Agnes' fainting. She had not counted on my presence in the stacks at that hour of the morning.

She had thought that Agnes would cry out, would come rushing back and that she herself would be the first on the scene of action or rather of inaction. No doubt she had planned to send Agnes for help while she herself, alone for a moment with the body, could hunt through Don's pockets for her letter. Every one in the library knew his habit of sticking letters into his pockets and leaving them there for days until there was no room for more.

But her scheme had miscarried. I remembered how silently she had followed Mr. Denman and me into the stacks. How baffled she must have felt looking down at that figure, unable to touch it. But later she had evolved another plan. She had returned to the stacks while I was alone there waiting for the return of Dr. Tyndale and Mark Denman. She had asked me then if I were going to search his pockets, probably expecting me to be sufficiently gallant to hand over to her unread that incriminating letter. A glance at the signature would have proved it to be hers. At my refusal she had darted forward, determined not to fail this time. But I had caught her wrists. A struggle, she knew, would avail nothing, would instead only call attention to a fact that she wanted obscured. She had submitted to my order as gracefully as possible.

But there was one thing more. She had already discovered the broken chain of her bracelet. Had she or had she not lost any of the links there in the library? The dropping of the handkerchief had been no accident. Before regaining it, she had wiped it across the floor at the exact spot where, a few moments before, I had picked up the links.

The excitement of my deductions had carried me back and forth across the floor innumerable times, but suddenly I was brought up short. Another shower of thoughts did much to dampen my convictions. I flung myself into an easy chair. Why were the two gold links (which had indubitably been part of the chain of the bracelet) located by the table eight feet from the body of Don Crawford? According to my calculations they should have been by the body, where indeed I had found another pair of links but ones which so far bore no connection with Bertha Chase or any of her possessions. If there had been a struggle during which the bracelet chain had been broken, then not the first links I had found but the second should have been located by the body. Twist it all as I might I could find no solution to the problem. I proceeded, therefore, to another point, the logic of which now seemed to me irrefutable.

Again I pictured Bertha Chase, guilty, baffled, but determined still. My previous supposition gained new strength as I reviewed it in the light of this new discovery. There must have been in the girl's mind the hope, or perhaps the fear, that Don Crawford, contrary to his usual custom, had not stuffed her letter into his pocket. She dared not search his room, but luck of a sort played into her hands. She had seen me in conversation with Agnes Hubbard, the girl with whom Don Crawford had been having a love affair. And she had seen me, after a word with this girl, disappear into the stacks. From some vantage point she had, no doubt, watched Agnes Hubbard follow me. Then — I was completely convinced of it now — she had gone outside the library and, hidden in the shrubbery near the basement stacks, she had overheard part of our conversation. Enough certainly to tell her of a manila envelope and the secret of its hiding place. Quickly then, without waiting to hear all our words, she had gone to the desk in the alcove and, following the directions she had just heard, had opened the secret aperture and procured the envelope. Again there was no time to investigate the contents. Later she had discovered her mistake, and had attempted that evening to return the envelope.

But why return it? Evidently she had not heard enough of our conversation to know its value. What was it she had reiterated there in the hospital? "Only a toy. Just something for a child."

But at the word "hospital" my thoughts received another jolt. Why, if Bertha Chase alone was guilty, had she met with an accident the preceding night? Why was the envelope clenched in her fingers, empty? What and who had struck her down? And why, as I had felt my way toward the switch box had I heard the quick breathing of two persons? I felt certain that Bertha Chase was implicated in the crime, that there was much that she could tell. But the events of the preceding evening indicated that others were involved. And it was plain that their purpose was not identical with her own. Here was a double mystery. I must begin to work from a new angle. As long as Bertha Chase lay unconscious in the hospital her secret was safe. But the original content of the envelope, the content that Don Crawford had thought valuable, was now in the hands of some one else. Who that person was and what the object was whose possession he had obtained were the two problems that now confronted me.

CHAPTER XIII

THERE were several leads left to follow. The only question was which to take first. As I thought over the possibilities, I realized that time was now one of the most important factors. This was Saturday — Senior Day. Sunday would be Baccalaureate and Monday, Commencement. If the other two suspects were students or alumni, Monday afternoon would find them far from the scene of the crime. I had to face the issue that if Bertha Chase was not the only guilty person, and the circumstances I had just reviewed seemed to support this view, then any one in the student body, on the faculty, among the hundreds of visitors, or any resident of the town might be implicated.

If Bertha Chase had murdered Don it was for one reason. If some one else was guilty, the motive was less certain. While admitting to myself that any one of hundreds of persons might be the criminal, I yet felt, more intuitively than reasonably, perhaps, that the circle of suspects was fairly small. If this were not so, the task was an impossible one, far worse than hunting for a needle in a haystack, which, I believe, often as it is mentioned, has never been attempted.

I say that it was mainly intuition that led me to limit the number of suspects. But there were in addition a few specific reasons that pointed to this conclusion. There was the matter of surroundings. Whoever had committed the crime was familiar with the library. I recalled the figure in the stacks on the previous evening when I had entered by the basement window. There had been a light suddenly extinguished. There had been the rapid ascent to the fourth level. Then later in the rotunda there had been the distinct sound of two people breathing rapidly as I fumbled my way toward the switch box.

Had one of them been Carla? I recalled that she had appeared suddenly at my elbow. She had, in fact, helped me unlock the switch box. But had she also helped that other dark figure to escape? Much as I hated to distrust her I was forced to admit the possibility. There was also her lurking suspicion of me.

I felt more and more convinced that I need not consider the hundreds of alumni and students. No stranger could know so intimately the arrangement and routine of the library. That narrowed the scope of my activities considerably. Now that numbers were disposed of, I thought of time, one of those twins that wait for no man. What persons who frequented the library would be leaving soon? One name immediately came to mind — Benjamin Morris.

Quite probably he would be taking his departure shortly after commencement.

A glance at a copy of the University Directory told me that he lived at the Rho Rho House. I lost no time in getting there. The fraternity house stood on an elevation well back from the street on Hillcrest Avenue. The smooth well-shaded lawn was dotted with groups of boys in various stages of undress. Some lolled around in pajamas, others were sun bathing with only shorts to preserve a slight untanned area. Benjamin Morris was one of the latter group, and after I had indicated my desire to have a word or two with him he led me to some lounging chairs in the shadow of a great elm. That he was ill at ease I could see at once, though certainly it was not because of his attire. The modern student has such complete *sang-froid* that when placed in company with a member of the faculty he exhibits usually far more poise than his elders. But now as he leaned forward to offer me a cigarette he dropped the pack on the grass. As he leaned down to retrieve them I thought what a handsome young god he was with his strong bronzed body and his red hair a tangle of light. Physically he was far more attractive than Don had been. Perhaps it was that quality which had swung the balance in his favor. But Don had had traits of mind and character which, in this lad, were as yet unproved. Perhaps Agnes Hubbard, with a woman's intuition, had detected propensities which I could not discern.

There were a few amiable preliminaries between

us which got us nowhere but which showed him surprisingly nervous for a lad who had been for the past four years one of the prominent figures on the campus. He flicked his cigarette ash too often and too quickly. I decided suddenly on a bold attack. Shilly-shallying would only put him on the defensive. My only hope was to surprise him into an admission.

"Morris," I said, "I have the unpleasant task of clearing up a few points before Commencement. Only complete frankness will help you." I knew this to be unfair, but I plunged on. "Just what were you doing in the stacks Thursday evening?"

"Thursday evening, why I wasn't—How could I have been there that evening?" His alarm was pathetic.

"That's what I'm asking you."

"What makes you think I was there? Why, good Heavens, that's the last place I'd choose for a frolic."

"But Agnes Hubbard says — " I hesitated. There could, of course, have been no continuation of my remark had my life depended on it.

A hurt and angry look swept over his face. "Oh! So it was Agnes Hubbard who saw me, was it? I should have thought I could count on her loyalty."

"Well now, Morris, since you've admitted it, you might as well come clean about the whole affair."

I watched the look of amazed alarm sweep over his face. It wasn't pleasant. The poor boy had spoken with such heat that he had not even realized he was betraying himself. But now he gathered his wits together.

"Not on your life," he said emphatically. "If you don't know what I was doing there, I'm safe. Do you think I'm going to spill anything just two days before I have the old diploma in my chubby fist? A fat chance!"

I was painfully aware that he was bluffing. Fear flickered wildly from his half-veiled eyes.

"Oh, all right if that's the way you feel. I just thought maybe I could help. You're rather in a spot you know. But maybe you'll be more willing to talk to the police."

"The police! But it's not a matter for them."

"I see that you don't realize the seriousness of the thing."

"But Mr. Allen, it can't be that serious. It's never been. The student faculty council handles all such cases."

A glimmer of light began to filter through to me.

"Just how drunk were you?" I asked.

"Oh, God, drunk enough to get the boot when it's found out. Is that what you're here for, to kick me out two days before Commencement?"

I felt suddenly omnipotent. "My boy," I said with my best academic manner of condescension. "I'll see that you're not kicked out if you'll tell me all you saw and did in the library that evening."

Instantly he became a fawning puppy in his gratitude.

"I'll tell you everything," he said eagerly. "A bunch of us went off together in the afternoon and got stewed, completely stewed. A rotten time of day to do it, too," he remarked as if that was the worst feature of the affair. "Anyway, coming back I got it into my head I wanted to clean up the office. That *was* a lousy idea, wasn't it?"

"Very," I agreed. "Especially at that particular time."

"Yes, it was just dinner time. I let myself in the library, and then I found I couldn't get upstairs. There's a spiral staircase, you know. And I was completely shot. So I went into the stacks and lay down. It was cool on the glass floor."

"Which level were you on?" I inquired.

"Oh, the first one I came to. The same level with the offices and reading rooms."

One flight above Don Crawford, I thought to myself.

"And how long were you there?"

"Till five-thirty the next morning. Then I woke up and streaked it back to the house. Crawled out one of the basement windows."

I remembered that I had found one open Friday morning.

"And did you hear anything while you were in the library, or see any one?" I pressed him.

"No, only once when a light flashed on, and I saw a woman in white standing there. Then it went off and I fell asleep again."

"And have you no idea who it was?"

"I didn't have then. But I suppose now it was Agnes Hubbard, since you say — "

"I said nothing. That was a low-down trick. She

didn't tell me a thing about your being in the stacks."

Instantly he was suspicious. "Just stringing me along, were you? I might have guessed it. And now that I've confessed, you'll tell the world." His tone was bitter.

"Don't be an ass. I'll tell no one. But some rather strange things went on in the library that night. It would help a bit if you had been conscious enough to notice and remember a few of them."

He looked startled. "Say, that was the night Mr. Crawford had his accident, wasn't it? I'd never thought of that before. You see I just passed completely out there on the floor."

So far as I could determine the boy was telling the truth. Either that or he was a remarkably good actor. And he had always impressed me as being a particularly ingenuous youth. As editor of the *Optima* he had made himself unpopular in certain undergraduate circles by his unceasing persecution of campus politics. With the zeal of the reformer he had sought to oust the so-called Liberal party in order to substitute for it the group he was sponsoring, called by him and his cohorts the Coalition party. So naïve had been his diplomacy and method of attack that I felt he could not now be lying. But in detecting a guilty person one must, I had always heard, suspect every one. And no matter how amateur the criminal was in this case (though I was beginning to think of him or her as a professional) I was, in my guise of detective, more amateur still.

There was nothing more to be learned from the

boy at present. "Well, if you recall anything," I remarked, "or if anything odd comes to your attention, I'd be glad if you'd get in touch with me."

He leaned forward suddenly and his voice was excited. "Say, you mentioned the police a minute ago. What's up anyway?"

"I don't know yet," I answered honestly enough. "But I'd be glad of your help. You're in and out of the library a good deal for one reason or another."

He smiled somewhat foolishly. Young love regards itself with as much embarrassment as seriousness. I thought with how much poise I should have maintained myself in the face of such an innuendo.

"If you see anything unusual going on, I'd be glad if you'd tip me off."

"I sure will," he said warmly, wringing my hand as I rose to go. "And here's hoping my sparklers light on something. You've been awfully decent to me, Mr. Allen."

"Well, keep everything to yourself," I warned him. I was arousing the suspicions of a good many people, I thought, and perhaps this was not the wisest course for me to take. On the other hand the frightened animal sometimes betrays itself in an attempt to run to cover. I walked along the street with a springy step. There is nothing a professor likes so well as the approbation of the critical class. I had done well, I concluded, in making an ally rather than an enemy of the boy.

It was getting late, but I had one more task to fulfill before meeting my dinner engagement with

Carla. I had remembered, as I talked with Benjamin Morris, that I had made no report to the office on the matter that had been my chief concern early Friday morning. Subsequent events had entirely blotted from my memory the plagiarized term paper. I must turn in an "F" for the semester grade of Thomas Morrow. I heartily disliked the necessity of doing so. Morrow was a good student, a Junior. He could easily have written a more than passable paper without the aid of minds better than his own. But I could not question the wisdom of the university regulations. I could only regret Morrow's foolishness in attempting such a piece of dishonesty.

As I filled out the requisite form I dismissed the matter entirely from my mind. I was to wonder later many times how many of all our tragedies in the library might have been averted had I but pondered long and earnestly on the subject of academic honesty or had I but whispered the one word "plagiarism" into the right pair of ears.

CHAPTER XIV

IT was seven o'clock when I stopped for Carla. We drove out about two miles on the lake road to North Bend Tavern. It is strange how a multiplicity of events can give an extension to time. It seemed a week since we had examined Bertha Chase's room together, and fully a month since I had found Don Crawford's body on the floor of the stacks. It was hard to realize that the discovery had been made only yesterday morning.

Carla looked rested. She had enjoyed another nap, she told me. She was wearing some sort of brown and white outfit that brought out the tawny tones of her skin and darkened her hair and eyes. I thought I had never seen her more alluring, and the knowledge that she preferred my company to that of the more experienced Mark Denman added a fillip to the occasion that caused my sprits to soar. What could she have in common with him, a cheap bounder, I thought, contemplating her serene loveliness across our small table on the terrace. But then I was forced to wonder, with almost a groan, what she could see in me, an unambitious pedagogue who was not sufficiently observant to solve a crime against his friend. I fear I was banal enough to voice part of this last thought to her.

"But you will solve it," she said. "I feel confident you will. And then you'll see what I have to say to you."

"And not before?" I asked.

"No, not before." Her voice was serious. So were her eyes, staring at me, dark and almost fearful in her lovely face.

What was it she feared? Was she anxious lest I make some discovery or lest I should not? Was she working with me or against me? She appeared to dislike Mark Denman. But was that only a clever pose? Had she been helping or hindering me last night in the dark library by the switch box? I must not let her know that I harbored the least suspicion of her, but I longed to be able to say to myself, "I trust her utterly."

Try as we might to keep our conversation away from the two days' events, our thoughts kept straying back to them and inadvertent remarks betrayed us to each other. Finally I gave up all pretense of steering the conversation toward books and theatres. I came also to a definite decision regarding my attitude toward Carla. With certain slight reservations I would take her into my confidence. I would assume that we were working toward the same objective, and we would do that work together. There were certain explorations and researches that I wanted to undertake. Very well, Carla should help me. She could not then be working behind my back, and if our mutual investigations showed her working at cross purposes, I would be in a position to discover it. I prayed that it was a discovery I should be spared.

Accordingly, as we watched daylight fade over the lake, I told her much of what I had learned in the past thirty-six hours. She listened attentively, voicing her amazement at times with low exclamations. I told her of the bruise on Don's chin, of the two sets of gold links I had discovered, of Bertha Chase's letter, of the document hidden in Agnes Hubbard's desk and of its disappearance.

"I simply can't believe it all," she said finally. "It doesn't sound real. But it's good of you to trust me." Her dark eyes were serious, but there was a mocking smile around her lips which I found it difficult to interpret.

She was silent and thoughtful for a few moments. Then she shook her head as if to dispel some bewilderment. "It doesn't fit," she said. "Don Crawford wasn't that sort of a person. Not the sort to be involved in a secret marriage or the sort to be murdered. It must have been an accident after all."

"It couldn't have been. I know he was killed." I had never felt so sure of it as at that moment. "And we have the letter to prove his marriage. Besides we know how desperately Bertha Chase tried to retrieve that letter."

"No." Carla shook her head. "You've put the puzzle together wrong. There's some big piece of it lacking that would change everything."

Did she speak from knowledge or intuition, I wondered.

"You'll never get anywhere until you discover what was hidden in Agnes Hubbard's desk," she continued.

"But how can we find that out?"

She shook her head. "I haven't the remotest idea," she confessed.

"Well, I haven't much more," I admitted. "But there is one circumstance that doesn't seem to belong anywhere. Who was the person in the stacks last night and what was he doing, taking books out of the shelves two sections away from where I found Don? If he's connected with the case at all that may be significant."

"Maybe something was hidden behind them."

"Yes, or in one of them. I've thought of that. But you must remember that it was fully half an hour after I saw the figure there that we found Bertha Chase lying on the floor of the alcove. And I feel sure that the document, the key to the whole situation, was taken from her then."

"Anyway I think we ought to go all over that section. Can't we do it to-night?" Carla looked at me eagerly.

It had been my very wish. Indeed I had planned to spend a good part of the night there and I had hoped to persuade Carla to accompany me. But at her suggestion I became suddenly fearful for her safety.

"It may be dangerous," I demurred. "We've no idea what we're up against."

"I'm not afraid." She smiled across at me. "Are you?"

"Only for you."

"Let's go then. I'll make a perfect Watson, I'm sure. Ask all the obvious questions and make asinine suggestions."

A few moments later we were flying along in "School's Out" as light-hearted as if we were launched upon nothing more hazardous than an exciting mystery movie.

It was about nine-thirty when we reached the library. We had stopped at Carla's house for the library keys and at mine for a couple of flashlights. Miss MacIntyre and Dr. Tyndale were talking on the porch as I dashed in and out of the house. They seemed inclined to engage me in conversation. I broke away from them a trifle rudely. Carla and I parked the car down a side street and hurried to the east entrance of the library. In certain spots the campus was brilliantly illuminated, but near the library the shadows were thick around the trees and shrubbery. Not a glimmer of light came from the building, and on the outside the only light was the one over the front entrance. I looked around for the night watchman, old Emil Schlachtman, but he was nowhere to be seen. Evidently he was keeping to schedule in his rounds this evening.

In complete darkness I inserted Carla's key and swung open the heavy door. The cool but musty air of the building engulfed us.

This side entrance was on a lower level than the

main doorway. It opened into a wide corridor leading to the reference reading room, located directly below the main reading room. To the right of the corridor, steps led upward, turning twice on broad landings and emerging on the main floor of the library near the door to the reading room. I handed one of the flashlights to Carla and turned on my own light. Stealthily we crept upward. Although nothing but the bare walls of the staircase confronted us, there seemed something strange and forbidding about the building. Our feet made furtive sounds on the stairs. As we emerged onto the main floor, the silence was thick about us, pricked by those small eerie creaks and crackings by which an empty building communes with itself. But were these truly sounds of emptiness? Elsewhere in the labyrinthine aisles and corridors were other figures skulking, intent on secret errands of their own? Carla's arm, which I had drawn through mine, began to tremble, and it was with an effort that I controlled my own muscles.

"Want to go back?" I whispered. Her quickly breathed "No" strengthened my own purpose. I flashed my light over the walls. We were in that portion of the building that extended at right angles from the semicircular main counter. Back of that counter or desk was the door into the stacks. We had previously decided not to turn on any lights until we had reached the portion of the stacks we wished to examine. Accordingly as we made our way forward through the darkness, I flashed my light down the narrow flight of steel stairs and preceded Carla to

the lower level. All about us hung a dead, close
silence. The air was stale and dry. I felt cold beads
of perspiration on my forehead.

Hand in hand we tiptoed down the rear aisle to
the section where, the night before, I had seen a figure
standing. I had counted the shelves accurately and
felt sure of the position. Carla snapped the button at
the end of the shelf, and the section was flooded with
light. In complete amazement I gazed at the case
before us. It was absolutely bare. The steel shelves
harbored not a single volume. Completely vacant,
they seemed to leer at us with a sort of toothless grin.
We stood there for a moment unable to believe the
evidence of our eyes. I had been prepared for a discovery of some sort, but not for the vacuity that now
confronted us.

"What shall we do?" whispered Carla.

"Nothing," I replied, speaking no louder than she.
It was strange that while we were supposedly alone in
the vast building neither us had raised his voice to
a normal tone since we had first slipped through the
side entrance.

As Carla turned off the light, I inadvertantly threw
my flash upward. What I saw held me motionless,
frozen with horror, the light still pointed above.
Carla moved to my side. I felt her quick breath on
my cheek. Within a few feet of our heads, outlined
clearly by the brilliance of my flashlight on the faint
greenish glass that was the floor of the next level, we
saw a long dark shadow. A body sprawled helplessly
on the floor above us, a quiescent body which to my

horror-stricken gaze seemed gruesomely similar to the body of Don Crawford.

It was only a moment that we stood there, but before I had lowered the light, sanity had returned to me. The arm flung out along the floor in so much the same attitude that Don's had been, moved slightly. The whole figure turned. Simultaneously we raced for the stairs, our two lights cutting circles of gold before us.

I snapped on two or three light buttons on the upper level. If any one was skulking in the darkness of those book-lined aisles, I had no intention of being surprised by his presence. It took us only a moment to reach the section where we had seen the body stretched out on the floor, and a great wave of relief swept over me as I gazed down at the startled face of Benjamin Morris. His eyes were open and he smiled at me rather ruefully. My expression evidently betrayed my suspicions, for he was the first to speak.

"Not this time," he remarked cheerfully. "Nothing stronger than water all day long."

He sat up and felt gingerly of the top of his head where a large bump was clearly manifest.

"Oh, boy, what a wallop that was!"

"Suppose you tell us what happened."

"As if I knew!" His grin was a bit sheepish. He got to his feet and bowed, rather too elegantly, I thought, to Carla. "I guess I'm the world's original nitwit," he said with becoming modesty. "But I got an idea in my head, and this is what it came to." He rubbed the unshapely eminence on his head.

"You see, sir," he continued more seriously, "I'd been thinking over what you said this afternoon. And on the way to Senior Banquet I got this sudden notion. I seemed to remember something about that woman in white I told you of."

He broke off suddenly. "Maybe I'd better wait and tell this to you later," he said looking meaningly at Carla.

"You need not fear to speak before Miss Robinson," I said with dignity.

"O.K. if you say so." He grinned with more understanding than I quite liked. I presume revenge is sweet to the undergraduate mind.

"Well, as I was saying, I seemed to remember a cane. So I thought I'd just hop in here a minute and see if I'd dreamed it, or if the lady really had a walking stick. Thought there might be some marks of it on the floor, you know. That was about eight-thirty. Say, what time is it now? I'll bet I'm late for the banquet."

"You are a trifle," I said. "But let's hear the rest of the story first. What happened?"

"I'd like to know myself. I found the cane marks, lots of them. You can see them all around here." He pointed to the floor. "The stick must have had a rubber tip. I was down on my hands and knees. Just started to get up. Didn't hear a sound or anything. Just a bang. Right on my cranium. That's the last I knew."

Carla drew her breath in sharply. "Let's get away from here," she said. "This place is giving me the creeps."

"Yes, I'd better get along myself," agreed Morris. "I suppose I've missed all but the speeches."

"Do you feel all right?" I asked him. "You've been unconscious quite a while."

"Fit as a fiddle," he assured me. "But I sure am a lousy detective."

"Suppose you and Miss Robinson go together," I suggested. "I'd like to look around here a bit."

But at this remark Carla objected strenuously and Morris himself became serious. "I don't think it's safe, Mr. Allen. Besides there are snakes here."

"Snakes!" Carla clutched my arm.

"Yes, I saw one on one of the shelves."

"That must have been Thursday night," I remarked grimly.

"No, sir, it was right here." He indicated a low shelf. But of course there was nothing there.

"Nonsense," I said. "But we'll all go if you think best. You go ahead and turn on the lights. I'll follow and turn them off after you."

They had got only as far as the door to the rotunda when without warning the entire building was plunged into utter blackness. The shock of it sent a thousand lurid fancies to my mind, and in the instant when the sound of our footsteps ceased I heard a faint clicking noise on the glass floor. Almost simultaneously came two other sounds that fairly curdled my blood—a terrified scream from Carla followed by the loud baying of a dog close beside me.

The flashlight was in my hand, and in its yellow circle I saw Carla shrinking against the door, one hand at her throat as if to stifle the scream already escaped. Beside me Emil Schlachtman's immense black dog cast a grotesque shadow over the fleeing figure of Benjamin Morris.

In a second I was beside Carla, and her shaky laughter alarmed me as much as had her sudden scream.

"I thought it was a snake," she said. "I put my hand on his tail. And the lights! But of course they always go off at ten."

The great dog stood quietly beside us, his furrowed face turned anxiously toward the glare of my light. The sharp clicking sounds drew nearer and the little Scotty, Napoleon, joined us.

"Come on," I said. "This is enough for one night." Docilely the two dogs followed us out of the building. Far across the campus we glimpsed the departing figure of our undergraduate hero.

CHAPTER XV

THAT night again I slept but little. Miss MacIntyre and Dr. Tyndale had both retired when I let myself into the house. A light burning in Dr. Tyndale's room told me he was reading late as was his custom. I envied him his peace of mind. Only a wall between us, and while he read with quiet contemplation I battled with fantastic phantoms of theory that led me nowhere. What would he say if I should knock on his door and inquire what his little Scotty was doing in the library this evening? It would be a useless interruption, I felt sure, for he paid small heed to the comings and goings of Napoleon.

I could probably answer the question better myself. No doubt when Emil Schlactman had made his eight o'clock rounds the two dogs had followed him into the library and when he left they had been locked in. Their appearance at the exact moment the lights had gone out had been uncanny. My blood chilled again at the remembrance of Carla's scream. No wonder Benjamin Morris had taken to his heels.

The snake he had seen had been the long black tail
of the hound swishing over the books as the dog made
his silent way through the stacks. He was a fearful
animal. I made a note to caution Emil Schlachtman
against letting him into the building. What if he
should slip into one of the girls' dormitories! What
a commotion he would cause!

Although the appearance of the dogs had been the
most gruesome event of the evening, it had been the
least significant. Far more alarming was the blow on
Benjamin Morris' head. What did that portend?
And the empty shelves of books. I berated myself
for an utter fool. What was the matter with me?
Events which must have some logical connection
were happening about me constantly, and I was always arriving a few moments or a few hours too
late. If I could only understand the sequence of
events. Somewhere in the maze of horror was the
thread that would unravel it all. If I could only
grasp it!

One thing I was determined upon. Somehow I
would run to earth that shelf of vanished books. The
advantage to me lay in their numbers. So many
volumes could not disappear into thin air.

Again that night my dreams were of books —
roomfuls of them that bayed like hounds at me when
I reached out to grasp them. I woke choking and
gasping in a room filled with bright morning sun-
shine.

My plan now was to obtain the assistance of Agnes
Hubbard. And after breakfast I directed my steps

toward the dormitory where she lived. Her expression of alarm at sight of me suffered a pleasing alteration when I explained my purpose.

"I want to find some books in the library," I told her, "and they are not in their proper place. I can't discover them and I wondered if you would be good enough to help. It will prevent your attending the Baccalaureate services this morning, but I have chosen that time to investigate because then every one will be in the auditorium."

"I'll meet you at the side entrance at quarter of eleven," she promised.

That allowed me a free hour which I employed in walking to the infirmary.

"She's just the same," Miss Johnson informed me. "No change at all. Dr. Whitaker left word that you were to be notified at the first indication of consciousness. We'll get in touch with you at the earliest sign."

I thanked her and continued my walk. If only Bertha Chase could talk! But would she if she could? If talking meant betraying herself she would be of no more use to me conscious than unconscious.

My stroll led me past the athletic field and down a dusty lane behind it. Here lying in front of a dilapidated shack I saw the two dogs that had caused so much consternation the night before. Napoleon certainly appeared oblivious to his surroundings. He seemed as much at home here as on the neatly clipped lawn in front of Miss MacIntyre's. This was undoubtedly the abode of Emil Schlachtman. A shabby kennel, almost as large as the shack, indicated that it was not necessity that led the great Dane abroad on nocturnal ramblings.

On a sudden impulse I went up the weedy path and knocked on the door. A night watchman must of necessity sleep in the daytime, and I was not surprised that it took several loud thumps before I heard footsteps approaching the door. I expected to see the tousled and probably angry face of Emil Schlachtman in the doorway, but it was a woman who stood in the opening. For some reason I had never imagined Emil Schlachtman as married, though I recalled now that he had mentioned grandchildren back in Heidelberg. So this forlorn creature with gray, unkempt hair and lost eyes was his wife. She stood there silently, clinging to the doorknob, fastening on my face her brown eyes, dull and lifeless.

"I beg your pardon," I said. "I just wanted to see Emil for a moment."

"He is asleep," she said tonelessly, with none of the accent that marked his every utterance.

"Will you give him a message for me, please, when he wakes? I'm Professor Allen of the university. Will you ask him to be careful not to let his dog into the college buildings?"

She looked at me blankly as if she had not understood a word I said. But from the room behind her came a loud snort. A few shambling steps brought Emil to the door. He looked dishevelled and sleepy. The sound of our voices had evidently roused him from his rest.

"Vos ist los?" he said in his gutteral voice. "Go, Anna."

I saw her cringe behind him into the shadows.

"Vat iss it, Provessor? You said somet'ing about Obie?"

"Yes," I replied. "I just stopped in to ask if you'd be a bit more careful to keep your dog out of the university buildings at night."

"Vat's dat?" He ran a hand through his rumpled hair. "Iss dat all you vake me up to say?"

"Yes, and it's plenty. How did your dog get in the library last night?"

"I nefer saw my dog all last night," he replied. Then suddenly he seemed to rouse himself. Drowsiness fled; his eyes glittered. "In der library, you say? Ach, ya, he must haf followed me in v'en I made my rounds." He gave a half chortling laugh and his blue eyes regarded me slyly.

A quick feeling of revulsion swept over me. In my previous encounters with the old man he had seemed a pathetic and somewhat picturesque figure. But now his curt dismissal of his wife and his appearance standing there dirty and disordered in his ramshackle hovel filled me with disgust.

"Well, be careful in the future," I said angrily. "Your dog nearly frightened Miss Robinson to death last night."

"Miss Robinson? So?" His eyes glittered at me evilly. "*Danke schön*, Provessor. I vill be more careful in der future, much more careful."

I fancied he was laughing at me as I picked my way along the dusty road.

The campus was deserted when I reached it again, and Agnes Hubbard was waiting inside the east doorway. I showed her the empty section in the stacks, and she jotted down the numbers at the side of the shelves:

FE
Ha 149
to
FE
He 162

We returned to the filing desk. "There are no cards for these books," she reported after a few minutes' investigation. "So no one can have taken them out, and if they were being repaired the cards would be here marked 'Mending.' We'll have to look in the general office."

She led the way across the rotunda to the room used by Mr. Denman and his assistants. It seemed to me that here a state of utter confusion reigned. Books of all sizes, catalogues and pamphlets lay piled on desks, counters and even chairs. The shelves of the room were laden.

"Annual renovation," explained Agnes. "It's not so bad as it looks." She progressed methodically from one corner of the room to the next. I hunted about rather aimlessly.

"Here they are," she announced pointing to a broad

table. I hurried to her side. "They're in here for relabelling. See, part of them have new markers on already. We varnish over the labels, you know. It's sort of queer, though," she continued in a puzzled thoughtful tone. "Not all of these old labels need renewing."

"Perhaps that's why only part of them are finished," I suggested rather inanely.

"No, otherwise they'd have been left in the shelves. We don't wheel books back and forth for the fun of it."

There were probably three hundred books on the table. I began to leaf through them.

"What are you looking for?" Agnes Hubbard asked curiously. "Can I help you?"

"Yes, I'd be glad if you would. It looks like quite a job. I'm looking for a pamphlet or some folded paper about the size of the contents of that envelope Don Crawford put in your desk."

She drew her breath in a long "O-o-oh. You're still hunting for that envelope, are you?"

"Not the envelope. Just the contents." I saw no need to tell her that the empty envelope was already in my possession. "I've a notion we may find something in one of these books."

But though we leafed through them all carefully, nothing unexpected came to our attention. I was grateful for Agnes Hubbard's assistance. Alone I could never have accomplished the task in the hour that it took us working together. But as I looked through the last book and shook open its pages, I

was no nearer a discovery than I had been when my
eyes first fell upon the empty shelves. Well, a bit
nearer. I qualified the thought a bit. Some one else
had evidently expected to find something here, had
perhaps already removed his discovery. Else why
had the entire lot of books been removed to this
office? And who had issued the order for their removal? There was but one answer to this query —
Mark Denman.

An idea struck me suddenly amidships. Was there
on this table every single volume that had been removed from those shelves?

I saw Agnes Hubbard glance surreptitiously at her
watch and I realized the lateness of the hour. It was
almost dinner time. Her desire to be off coincided
with my wish to be left alone for a few minutes in
the library. My thanks were profuse as I escorted
her to the door.

"Of course I don't want this mentioned," I said.
She eyed me soberly.

"But if you see Benjamin Morris you might ask
him about his latest adventure in the stacks. Tell
him I said he could tell you to the last detail."

She glanced at me nervously, and when I laughed
she looked relieved but puzzled. I wondered just
how successfully Benjamin Morris would gloss over
the facts of his ignominious flight.

With the closing of the door behind her I hurried back to the book-laden table. The volumes were
arranged in alphabetical order. It took me only a
moment to discover that there was indeed one book

missing. FE rested on FE   And nowhere on the
    Ha 345   Ha 347·
table could I discover a volume labelled FE
                        Ha 346·

I wasted no time in looking around the littered
room. If the book was gone it was no mischance that
had mislaid it. The person who had ordered the
books brought up to the office had obtained the volume he was seeking. In four steps I crossed to Mark
Denman's desk. It was locked of course. But the
golden oak desks which the university provides
have locks of a strikingly similar design. I had the
identical twin to this roll top desk in my office in
Chamberlin Hall. The key was in my pocket. I inserted it carefully in the lock. The top rolled up
quietly.

There before me, completely unconcealed, resting
on innumerable papers, was the volume I sought.
I noted its exact position before I removed it. Then
I leafed hurriedly through its pages. Nothing was
concealed there. He had got ahead of me then. Whatever had been hidden there had been removed. But
why then had he not replaced the book in its proper
position on the table? I leafed through it again more
carefully. Suddenly my eyes nearly popped from my
head. In the narrow inner margin of a page about
halfway through the book I saw writing. Before I
had read a word I had recognized the infinitesimal
lettering of my friend Don Crawford. With increasing
astonishment I read what was written there. It
seemed like a voice from the dead, but a voice speak-

ing of those ridiculous matters which, in spiritual manifestations, the dead so often choose to remark upon. I had been to a seance once when the returned spirit devoted all his time and ours to a description of the games he and his friends played in their new environment.

Now these words of Don Crawford's stared up at me like so much meaningless nonsense.

"The knave also knows value of Queen's ♡ . Must I share with him? Decidedly no. Behold I am threatened!"

The writing broke off, and a long thin pencil mark trailed weakly down the page.

What had Don Crawford been trying to say? I knew his eccentric habit of holding a pencil in his hand while conversing. As some people sit at the telephone making dots and circles on a pad, so he jotted down words and fragments of the conversation in which he was engaged. It was a habit acquired during his note-taking days in college, and much as I ridiculed the practice, he did not discontinue it.

I felt no doubt now that the words at which I was gazing referred to a conversation — probably his last, for the pencil had trailed off into an ominously faint line after the words, "Behold I am threatened!" But the rest of the notation sounded like so much gibberish to me.

I do not know how many minutes I sat staring down at the words, completely lost to my surroundings. But suddenly I became conscious of voices. Footsteps sounded on the stairs leading from the east entrance. I had not a minute to lose. Hastily I replaced the book in the position in which I had found it. Quietly then I rolled down the top of the desk and locked it. The footsteps were ascending the stairs rapidly. Two people were laughing. I recognized their voices — Carla's and Mark Denman's. I gave a despairing look around me. There seemed no place to hide and I had small wish to be apprehended. Perhaps they would not come into this office. I slipped to the floor behind a broad counter. It was not till then that I noticed that the counter was hollow. About three feet high and two wide, its interior was evidently used for storage purposes. A sliding door gave entrance. I crawled inside the dusty cave and slid the door almost shut. I was none too quick.

"I won't be a minute." I could hear Carla's voice, gay and excited, as she stood in the rotunda by the door opening into the office where I was hidden. "I'll just run up and leave my cap and gown in the office."

Then Mark Denman's heavy tread sounded in the room. I felt perfectly safe in my dark hole under the counter, but my heart was beating hard and fast. What if Denman discovered that his desk had been tampered with? Had I replaced the book in the exact position in which I had found it?

But his steps did not approach the desk. I applied an eye to the inch-wide opening left by the sliding door. He was fumbling among some large books on a high shelf. He pulled out one of them, a large paper-bound volume.

Something was crawling on my neck. It was with the greatest restraint that I avoided slapping it. My fingers closed on a large spider. Heaven only knew how many more lurked in the corners ready to pounce upon me.

Mark Denman's steps came back to his desk. Now he was sliding the top up. Evidently he noticed no change. I screwed my head around to an uncomfortable angle. Through the tail of my eye I could just glimpse him dropping the large paper-bound volume on his desk. Quietly he rolled down the top. I heard the key click. He walked quickly to the door.

"Lovelier than ever," I heard him say. "Carla, you're a vision with that ray of light dropping down on you."

So he called her "Carla." I longed to punch his nose. But I remained quiet and squeezed the life out of another spider.

"Don't be silly." Her voice sounded happy. "We'll have to hurry if we want to get any dinner. The place will be crowded to-day."

In unison their footsteps receded toward the side entrance. I remained with the spiders until I heard the outer door bang.

"The knave!" Was that Denman? "The Queen's heart?" Did that mean Carla's? But no, of course not. She was not Don's Queen. That would be Agnes Hubbard, and in that case the knave could be only

Benjamin Morris. Had the lad deceived me after all? Had his presence in the stacks been less somnolent than he would have me believe?

I crawled out of my cave and stooped for a few moments on the floor dusting the cobwebs from my clothes and listening to be sure that I was again alone. There was complete silence. By now Carla and Mark Denman were hastening to some tea room. I felt my hard-won confidence in her crumbling.

But there was no time to lose. At almost any moment some one else might enter the building. I must work fast. Again I approached the desk, turned the lock, rolled up the top.

I played in luck. The large paper-bound volume was a book catalogue. Its cover bore the words:

A SELECTION OF
BOOKS MANUSCRIPTS ENGRAVINGS
AND AUTOGRAPH LETTERS
REMARKABLE FOR THEIR INTEREST &
RARITY
BEING THE
FIVE HUNDREDTH CATALOGUE
ISSUED BY
MAGGS BROS.
BOOKSELLERS
BY APPOINTMENT   TO HIS MAJESTY
KING GEORGE V
LONDON
MAGGS BROS.
34 and 35 Conduit Street, London, W.C.
1928

I turned the pages eagerly. A slip of paper marked two of the leaves, and on one of them, page number 156, I read something that made me catch my breath.

93. LAMB (CHARLES): KING AND QUEEN OF HEARTS, 1805.
THE KING AND QUEEN OF HEARTS, SHOWING HOW NOTABLY THE QUEEN MADE HER TARTS, AND HOW SCURVILY THE KNAVE STOLE THEM AWAY; WITH OTHER PARTICULARS BELONGING THEREUNTO.
With 15 Engravings, uncoloured, as issued. THE EXCESSIVELY RARE FIRST EDITION. *12mo.* IN THE ORIGINAL BLUE PRINTED WRAPPERS (*back slightly repaired*).
LONDON, PRINTED FOR THOMAS HODGKINS AT THE JUVENILE LIBRARY. 1805.
(*See Illustrations opposite and overleaf*)   £1500
THE FIRST ISSUE OF THE FIRST EDITION.

THE ONLY COPY KNOWN HAVING THE WRAPPER DATED 1805. There were five issues of this book. The plates were engraved in 1805, but only a very few copies were issued that year. When the call came for copies in the following years a new wrapper was printed with the new date — hitherto the 1806 edition had been considered the earliest; and Livingston, in his Bibliography of Lamb, gives 1806 as the first issue, but remarks: "It is possible that copies were issued having this date 1805 on the cover."
This, the first of Charles Lamb's Books for Children, is so excessively rare that no copies were known until one was discovered by E. V. Lucas in 1901, and since then only one or two have come to light.

I sat for some moments staring at the page and at the illustrations on the two succeeding pages. They represented the covers and two engravings of the 1805 edition. So many things were clear to me now, and yet so much remained to be discovered. I must sort out my information and weigh it against this new disclosure. But first a spirit of mischief took hold of me. Whipping out my knife I carefully cut the two pages from the catalogue. I might need them later. And I liked to imagine the expression on Mark Denman's face when he discovered the loss.

It was important now that my presence in the library should be known to no one. Accordingly I resorted again to the basement windows of the stacks and emerged innocently enough on a campus devoid of human beings. The whole town was intent apparently on feeding the inner man. I joined them in the pursuit, in the clean but unæsthetic atmosphere of George and Harry's.

CHAPTER XVI

BUT I was not content merely to eat. Amid the bustle of changing plates my thoughts arranged themselves. I knew now what Don Crawford's valuable discovery had been. He was forever ordering books. In some miscellaneous shipment one really rare document must have come into his hands. I had no doubt that he had discovered himself to be the possessor of an 1805 copy of Lamb's essay. According to the catalogue the one extant copy was valued at £1500. To possess a second copy which would bring approximately that amount would mean everything to Don Crawford. Six thousand dollars would be a fortune to him. What was it he had said to me? "It would give me leisure to complete my book." I realized that, with his frugal habits, six thousand dollars would have bought him several years of freedom.

But what about Bertha Chase? Would she not have demanded her share of her husband's money? Had he planned to desert her? It was strange to think that she had had the book in her possession and had been ignorant of its value. I was more positive than ever now that it was she who had removed it from Agnes Hubbard's desk. Her words, "Only a toy. Just something for a child," were understandable in the light of my new discovery.

But where was the book now? The evidence in his desk seemed to point to Mark Denman. But it might be that he only knew of its existence and wanted to get his hands on it.

Was the desire for six thousand dollars a sufficient cause for murder? I had to admit that to most people, fortunately, it would not seem so. But the standards of value, financially speaking, of the outside world are far different from those of a college community. In these days of depression when most professors' salaries averaged between two and three thousand dollars, the immediate conversion of a small pamphlet into six thousand dollars of cold cash might be a temptation. Especially would this be true if there were an immediate need for money. Few college professors have investments or savings other than insurance. I wondered if Denman had been playing the stock market.

Don's pencilled notation became understandable now. The Queen's heart referred, of course, to the copy of the essay. The knave — was that Denman? And the concluding four words, "Behold I am threatened!" Threatened by whom — by the knave or by Bertha Chase whose letter in itself had been a threat?

The pieces still didn't fit together. By rights Bertha Chase should have known the worth of the booklet. But I was convinced that she had not. And Don's tragic death. Had it been a crime of passion or of greed? Well, I was collecting more pieces. Get enough of them and they must fit together some way, I told myself.

I still had two unidentified gold links. And there was the tall woman in white — and her cane. Had Benjamin Morris only dreamed or imagined that? Could nothing but a rubber-tipped cane have made those round marks on the glass floor? But there was the corroboration of the night watchman. Emil Schlachtman also had seen a tall women in white, and she had disappeared into the shrubbery. By some means I must identify her. I did not dream how soon or how easily she would step into the picture.

I paid my bill and went out of the restaurant. My walk home led me past the Tea Kettle Inn. Carla and Mark Denman were just emerging. Her greeting was light-hearted in the extreme. I bowed coldly, unable to overlook the triumphant expression of Mark Denman's handsome face. My heart was heavy, but I smiled to myself as I thought of the page from Catalogue Number Five Hundred of Maggs Brothers that lay folded in my pocket.

The festive air of Commencement time lay over the village. Up and down the elm-shaded streets wandered groups of alumni and of Seniors with their relatives. Introductions were plentiful. I was stopped many times to meet fathers and mothers who beamed proudly at the achievements of their offspring. There is something pitiful in the vicarious sense of triumph with which parents regard the diplomas of their children. "I never had a chance to go to college myself, but I was determined that my children should have the opportunity." How many times I heard that remark as I made my interrupted progress toward Miss MacIntyre's house! I could only hope that these graduates would justify the sacrifices of their families.

I passed Benjamin Morris surrounded by a group of people whose family resemblance proclaimed them to be fond relatives. He grinned at me rather sheepishly, but made no move to stop me. I was interested to note that Agnes Hubbard was talking animatedly with an older woman whom I judged to be Benjamin's mother. That affair seemed to be progressing successfully. Of course Agnes was loyalty personified. I thought ruefully of Carla.

Miss MacIntyre's shady lawn looked peaceful and inviting. I contemplated a nap and decided in favor of it. My subconscious might do something for me in the realm of sleep. My deductive faculties certainly needed some sort of assistance.

However, as I stepped into the wide, cool hallway, all my plans were disrupted. From the old-fashioned front parlor at the right, the figure of Miss MacIntyre fairly flew at me.

"Oh, it's you, Professor Allen." The disappointment in her voice was almost a sob. I saw that she was shaking.

"What is it, Miss MacIntyre? Are you in trouble?" I led her to a large chair in the parlor. I saw, now that my eyes were adjusted to the dimness of the interior, that she had been crying.

She seemed pitifully shrunken from her usual erect self. Her stiffly starched white lawn dress was like a shell inside of which she cowered. She shook her head, biting her lips. "I mustn't tell," her old voice quavered.

"But you're frightened," I said. "Can't I help you?"

"No, I don't know what you could do. There's nothing you could do." She dabbed at her eyes.

"Come," I said pulling up a chair beside her and taking one of her hands in mine, "try me out. I'm sure I can help."

For a moment she shrank farther into her stiff high-necked dress. Then she turned timidly toward me, her eyes swimming. "It's about Dr. Tyndale," she quavered. "He hasn't been home to dinner."

If her tearful eyes had not been looking directly at me, I should have given vent to the mirth that struggled for expression. But with her concerned face turned to mine, I could only smile reassuringly and pat her hand.

"Why, that's nothing," I said. "He's probably been invited out to dinner somewhere and forgotten to tell you."

"He never forgets."

"Well, some old friend probably picked him up after Baccalaureate and took him off to dinner. He'll turn up in a little while. Don't worry."

"No," she said emphatically, sitting up straighter

and taking her hand from mine, "you don't understand. He wouldn't do that. He knows that I'd worry."

"But why should you worry? He's all right."

"No, he's not. I've been so worried ever since — " She stopped suddenly. The tears stood in her eyes again.

"Ever since what?" I asked gently.

"I shouldn't tell you." Her voice was a half whisper. "But I can't stand it alone any longer. I've been so anxious ever since he was threatened."

"Threatened!" I almost shouted the word. "How could he be? Who could possibly threaten him?"

"I don't know," she said, and now her voice was steady. It was as if, relieved of her secret, she had regained her composure. It was my turn now to be disturbed.

"When did it happen?" I asked. "How long has it been going on?"

"It happened a week ago to-morrow," she said, "on last Monday. Somebody telephoned. It was a woman's voice. Not a lady's, you know, a woman's. I didn't mean to listen but I couldn't help hearing part of what Dr. Tyndale said. He shouted so. He seemed very angry. He said, 'What?' several times, and finally just before he hung up he said, 'Very well, I'll be there at nine.'"

"I was here when he came in about ten. He didn't stop as he usually does. Sometimes I make him a cup of cocoa, you know. He just said 'Goodnight' and went up to his room. But oh, the way he looked."

Miss MacIntyre buried her face in her hands a moment before she continued.

"He looked awful — so old and frightened. I'd never seen him look that way. And then I heard him walking back and forth, back and forth, for hours up there in his room. Why, you must have heard him too; didn't you? You have the room next his."

"I was at the Faculty Club till late," I reminded her. "Everything was quiet when I came in."

"It's been going on ever since," she continued, hardly noticing my reply. "Telephone calls and letters, and one night some one came here. I saw Dr. Tyndale in the garden near the alley talking to some one. It frightened me and I went out there. They must have heard me, for Dr. Tyndale was alone when I reached him. But I heard that same woman's voice."

"What did she say?" I asked eagerly.

"She warned him. I was closer than they thought perhaps, for I heard the woman say, 'You must be careful. Do just as he says. He'll end your life here if you don't.'"

Miss MacIntyre sank back exhausted, staring at me with terror which her own words had evoked.

I felt my spine prickle. Here was another part of the puzzle as ill-matched as all the others. Who could be threatening the old man? Had Don Crawford also been warned of his danger? And was Dr. Tyndale to be the next victim?

"What night was it you saw the woman in the alley?" I asked her.

She passed a trembling hand over her eyes for a

moment. "It was early Thursday evening," she answered, her voice a mere quaver of sound.

Then with an effort she roused herself. "But something's happened to him now," she said. "I know it. Something awful's happened to him. You'll have to go and find him."

"Perhaps he's in his office," I said. "Had you thought of that?"

"Yes, but I can't go there. I've been frightened of the library since — "

She stopped, looking at me fearfully. I longed to remain and question her, but I knew this was not the time. Her present fears must be soothed before I could learn more. But as I hurried toward the library, I knew as surely as if she had told me that she was the tall woman in white.

As I neared the building, I saw groups of people gathered on the steps. A sudden nameless fear gripped me. I thought of that shaken old lady in her high-ceilinged front parlor. Then I realized that so far no tragedy had occurred. The library was simply open to the inspection of the college guests. I could see them moving slowly in and out of the doors. Their presence seemed to restore normalcy to the building which since Friday morning had grown increasingly sinister to me.

The route to Dr. Tyndale's office led me up the spiral staircase and past Carla's door. I had no expectation of seeing her there. It must have been the steep stairs and the rate at which I ascended them that caused the thumping of my heart.

But she was locking her office door as I came along. "Hello," she said airily, "you're the very person I want to see."

"Indeed?" I responded.

She wasted no time. "Don't be silly. I'm making marvellous progress."

"So I've noticed."

"Well, meet me here at nine o'clock and I'll prove it," she said defiantly. "You'll see then what's happened to the Queen's tarts."

And at my stare of incredulity she laughed and ran down the stairs.

"Carla," I cried, but she waved a hand and disappeared.

What was she up to? I felt angry, bewildered, worried. But I had no time for self-pity. I was here to find Dr. Tyndale. And just as I had foreseen, he was perfectly safe. He stood just inside his open doorway talking to Agnes Hubbard and Benjamin Morris. He had a hand on the shoulder of each. Evidently giving them his blessing. With a curt nod I passed them and, rather than retrace my steps, descended the staircase in the stacks.

A wild goose chase, I thought to myself, and what had it netted me? Only the baffling laughter of Carla, who seemed, after all, to be more interested in Mark Denman than in me. She could go off with him for the day, could she, and then expect me to run at her bidding to keep a nine o'clock appointment? At that hour, I was resolved, I should be getting a much needed rest.

I was a bit out of patience by the time I reached

the gate of Miss MacIntyre's house. But the sight of her standing in the doorway, wringing her hands, brought back a flood of pity for the lonely old lady. Poor soul, with so few interests and so restricted a life. I was glad it was good news I was bringing her. The wave of relief that swept over her face when I assured her of Dr. Tyndale's safety was pathetic to witness. Her tense figure relaxed suddenly, and I half carried her to a sofa in the front parlor.

She lay there a moment with her eyes closed. Then she smiled up at me. "You're very good to me," she said faintly. A worried little line appeared on her forehead. "But I wonder why he didn't come home to dinner. You will continue to watch over him for me, won't you?"

This, I saw, was the time to question her. "I will," I promised. "But first you must tell me everything you know. You were in the library Thursday evening, weren't you? What did you see there?"

She drew a long quivering breath. But in the next instant she was sitting erect on the sofa and her voice was firm when she answered.

"I should have told before," she replied. "But I've been so afraid. I saw that young man in the stacks Thursday evening. He must have been dead then. But I didn't know it. I thought he was asleep. And I was so relieved that it wasn't Dr. Tyndale. You see I was looking for him. I was afraid for him. He'd slipped out of the house when I had callers. I think that poor young man was killed by mistake. I think it was Dr. Tyndale she was after."

"She?" I asked. "What do you mean by 'she'?"

"Oh, I forgot I hadn't told you. I saw her there beside him in the stacks Thursday evening. Not to recognize. It was dark. But I could see her figure quite clearly. She wore a white dress. Then she just glided away. I must have knocked my cane against something. I was carrying my father's old cane. In order to be armed, you know."

"Poor old soul," I thought. "What protection would a cane be in those frail, veined hands?"

"But you must have been very close," I said. "Didn't you see her face at all?"

"No, I wasn't close," she replied. "I was at the far end of the aisle and her back was toward me. She was kneeling beside him there at the table."

"At the table!" I could not repress my shout.

Miss MacIntyre looked startled. "Oh," she cried, "I never thought of that. Yes, it was by the table. And he was found on the floor, wasn't he? Then he wasn't dead when I saw him. I could have saved him."

"Perhaps not," I said. "Perhaps he was dead when you saw him. How did he look?"

"He looked asleep or — or — intoxicated." She glanced at me timorously. "I walked up and turned my flashlight on him. I thought it might be Dr. Tyndale, you see."

"You were very brave."

"No, not brave. Just frightened. Then I saw his light hair. His arms were spread out on the table and his head was down on one arm. I just tiptoed away."

"But why did you think he was drunk?"

"I saw another young man upstairs who was. He was lying on the glass floor. I could smell his breath."

I had a mental picture of her tiptoeing over those glassy floors, a flashlight in one hand, a cane in the other. How fear must have stalked at her elbow! How terrified she must have felt as she looked down at Don's figure, fearing for the second time that she had found the lifeless form of the man she sought. At any rate her story verified that of Benjamin Morris. He really had "passed out" there on the floor of the stacks as he had told me. And the figure in white had been no product of his imagination. I stared at Miss MacIntyre in amazement, and a fear grew within me. Had she also been in danger of death that evening, this gentle, anxious lady whose worry had led her up and down those haunted aisles? The woman kneeling beside Don Crawford! That could have been none other than Bertha Chase. Did she realize that she had been seen? And Don's body! How had it reached the floor of the end aisle where I had found it?

"How long were you in the library" I asked her. "And did you find Dr. Tyndale?"

"I must have been there half an hour," she replied calmly. "I looked everywhere. But he wasn't there."

"And how did you get in?" I asked her, though I thought I knew the answer. That white figure disappearing into the shrubbery!

"Through the basement window," she replied. "I used to go in that way years ago when I was a girl." Some memory of far-gone days touched her eyes with light. Then she continued. "I came out that way, too. And when I came home there was Dr. Tyndale on the porch. He'd just been for a walk."

Just as I had, I thought. It had been a lovely, warm, starry night. But his thoughts that evening, I would venture to say, had not been so romantic nor so foolish as my own.

Miss MacIntyre looked at me wistfully. "I feel better now that I've told you," she said. "But that poor young man! Do you think I could have saved him?"

"I don't know," I replied. "But I think not. He was probably dead when you saw him."

Dead, I thought, with his last message written in a book that had somehow been replaced in the shelves.

"And the morning?" I asked. "Why did you return in the morning?"

"Why, Dr. Tyndale — " she began, but she got no further.

"Yes?" said a voice in the doorway. "Did you call me?"

We had neither of us heard him enter the house, so intent had we been on our conversation. He came forward now, his tall figure bent slightly, peering at us in his nearsighted way.

"I'm afraid I forgot about dinner," he said apologetically. "I had an appointment at my office."

And as I looked at him I knew that he was lying. He had not forgotten his meal. His mouth hung lax and quivering. Suddenly all that Miss MacIntyre had told me was corroborated. Here before me stood a man in deadly fear of his life. Perhaps Don Crawford's death *had* been a ghastly error.

CHAPTER XVII

THE rest of the afternoon passed quietly. Miss MacIntyre led Dr. Tyndale back to the screened-in kitchen porch to give him his belated meal. I went up to my room where I rested for the remainder of the afternoon. I threw myself upon the bed where, between fitful naps, I tried to get some sense and order out of the new angles of the case. There were now two quite definite points to be clarified. Until Bertha Chase talked and until I discovered who was threatening Dr. Tyndale, I felt I could make small progress toward a solution. It would be useless, I knew, to question the old scholar, for he was noted for his taciturnity. My best method there would be to keep a close watch on him as Miss MacIntyre had requested. It would be equally futile for me to scurry around the campus or hunt through the library for the 1805 copy of Lamb's essay. By watching and waiting I would be doing all that was now possible.

I finally fell into a deep sleep which would probably have carried over to the next day had I not been roused by an insistent knocking on the door. I came awake slowly, confused as to the time, bewildered to find myself completely dressed. Twilight was fingering its way into the room.

Miss MacIntyre's gentle voice came to me from the hall. "Mr. Allen, Mr. Allen, you're wanted on the telephone."

I stumbled to my feet. "It's important, they say." She turned away.

In an instant I had caught up my coat, thrown open the door, and dashed past her down the stairs.

"It's Miss Manning from the hospital," came a clear voice over the wire. "Can you come immediately?"

"At once," I replied. And without returning to my room I hurried from the house and down the street toward the infirmary.

Dr. Whitaker's car was standing in the driveway when I arrived. Miss Johnson met me at the door. "She's talking a lot," she said, "though she seems quite irrational. She doesn't recognize any of us."

"Should she know you?" I asked.

"Oh, yes, she was here for a week in the winter with the flu. She ought to remember us. Dr. Whitaker's with her now," she continued as we approached the door to Bertha Chase's room.

The patient's voice was raised. It echoed weirdly down the vacant corridor and as I distinguished the words my blood turned cold.

"I want my husband. I want my husband," she repeated. "Darling, please come to me. I'm sick. Don't you see? I feel so sick and I need you."

Then Dr. Whitaker's voice trying to soothe her. "Don't worry; he's busy now. But he'll come presently. Do you want to send him a message?"

"No, only to come to me. Only to hurry."

The doctor saw me standing at the door and beckoned me to enter. "Who is her husband?" he whispered.

But before I had time to answer, Bertha Chase turned her eyes to my face. An utterly lovely smile transformed her expression. She held out her hands. "Darling, I knew you would come." Her glance did not waver from my face.

I could see Dr. Whitaker and the two nurses exchange surprised glances, but to deny the delusion of the sick girl was beyond my power as I gazed down at her transfigured face. I sat down in the chair drawn up beside the bed and took the girl's hands in mine. Dr. Whitaker stood beside me. The two nurses were at the foot of the bed, but Bertha Chase seemed oblivious to all but my presence.

"I knew you'd come," she said happily. "I've had such a lovely dream. I dreamed you still loved me. And you do, don't you?"

There seemed for a moment nothing I could say. And as I looked at her in silence, an expression of panic dawned in her eyes and deepened. I felt Dr. Whitaker's hand pressing my shoulder. "Of course — of course I love you," I gulped.

A wave of relief swept over her face. "I knew you did. I've known ever since Friday. If you hadn't loved me you wouldn't have tried to protect me, would you, darling? I saw you put that book back into place."

Under Dr. Whitaker's hand I felt my shoulder twitch. What revelations were about to follow? The doctor signalled to the nurses. They slipped quietly away, though at the door Miss Manning looked back curiously at us. It must have been a strange tableau.

The happy voice continued. "And I protected you too, dearest. I never told a thing. But I can't understand it. Why did you move his body away from the table? Why did you do it, Mark?"

My heart stopped beating for a moment. Then its heavy thudding seemed to shake my body. Dr. Whitaker's hand felt like a vise on my shoulder. There was utter silence in the little room.

"Answer me," she said suddenly. "Why did you move him? I've been so worried. Oh, Mark, I can't help it if I'm the worrying kind of wife."

My head was whirling. But I knew I must keep her talking. She would tell me things as long as she thought I was her husband — as long as she thought I was Mark Denman. So it hadn't been Don Crawford at all. What a fool I had been ever to suspect him of that.

"Suppose you tell me your side of it first," I suggested. "Then I'll tell you mine. I've been worried, too."

"Have you, Mark?" she smiled at me. "I love to have you worry about me. Did you worry about the way I tried to vamp Don Crawford?"

Dr. Whitaker made a quick movement, and for the first time she seemed to realize his presence.

"Who is that?" she asked fearfully.

"Just the doctor," I said, smoothing her hand.

"But I can't talk before him." Her eyes appealed to me.

"I'm just going, Miss Chase," Dr. Whitaker volunteered. He tiptoed from the room, but I knew he would remain outside the open door listening.

Bertha Chase giggled. "Isn't it funny? It's made me laugh for weeks to be called Miss Chase when I'm really Mrs. Denman. Especially when that awfully proper Mr. Allen speaks to me. He's such a prig."

I felt the blood in my face. "But tell me about Thursday night," I said. "Why were you in the library?"

"I was hunting you," she said. "And I saw you too. With that Carla Robinson up in her office. I wanted to talk to you. You see I'd written you a letter and you hadn't answered it."

In her illness Bertha Chase talked like a child. I felt sure that in her right mind she never would have revealed to Mark Denman the things she was relating to me under the mistaken impression that I was he. Her mind seemed perfectly uninhibited. I recalled Dr. Whitaker's words, "Concussion does queer things."

She smiled up at me gently. "I was awfully jealous. I've known for a long time you were crazy about her, and it's made me wild."

I felt a rush of sympathy for the girl.

"When I saw you both come out of her office, I slipped around back to the staircase into the stacks. I was excited and I must have gone down one flight too many. I meant to come out on the main floor and follow you, but I was on the floor below. And then I saw Don Crawford. He was sitting by the table with his head on his arms. I thought he was asleep. And I thought I'd wake him and ask if he'd delivered the letter I'd asked him to give to you. I wanted to know if you'd said anything when he gave it to you.

"He didn't rouse when I spoke his name, so I shook him a little. That didn't rouse him either. His head just flopped to one side. I knew then something was the matter. Then I saw a manila envelope sticking out of his pocket. I thought it was my letter to you and that he had forgotten to deliver it. I pulled it out. Then I heard some one coming and I slipped out and went home."

"But it wasn't your letter after all, was it?" I asked.

"No, it wasn't." She looked at me suspiciously a moment. "How did you know?"

"I only guessed. I thought maybe it was a note from Miss Robinson. She said she'd written me one that I never got." I felt that I was playing my part well, guilefully and diplomatically too.

"The hateful creature!" Bertha Chase's features were contorted with rage. "But you called her 'Miss Robinson.' " She almost crowed with delight.

I gave her hand a brief squeeze.

Her expression grew serious. "But, Mark, why did you move the body?" she asked. "And why did you kill him?" Her voice sank to a whisper, but a penetrating whisper which I was sure found its way to the doctor standing by the door in the hall.

"What makes you think I did kill him?" I deplored the use of the first person, but I saw no other way to continue her delusion.

"Because you were jealous." A smile of complete satisfaction wreathed her face. I felt all my old dislike for the girl sweep back, strengthened a hundredfold.

"I wanted to make you jealous," she continued. "But I thought you didn't even notice. I didn't know you would be that angry."

There was no horror in the expression of her face, only gratification and a queer kind of triumph.

"But don't worry," she said. "I won't betray you. You tried to protect me there in the alcove, didn't you? I recognized your step. But what happened? I can't remember."

She had recognized Mark Denman's step in the alcove! Then he was one of the figures who had dashed past me there in the dark. Now I had only to find the other.

"Some one must have struck you," I said. "Or perhaps you lost your balance."

She put a hand to her head. "I heard a step," she began. Then suddenly her eyes closed and she was asleep, her hand resting lightly on mine. As gently as possible I released my fingers. I tiptoed to the door. Dr. Whitaker summoned Miss Johnson. Then he and I stepped into the waiting room.

"What do you make of it?" I asked him eagerly.

"I don't know what to think." Dr. Whitaker sank heavily into a chair. "Of course it may all be a delusion. She may have everything twisted in her mind, just as she has you confused with Mr. Denman. All that she's been saying may be just what she has imagined or dreamed during the past two days."

"No," I replied. "It can't be altogether imaginary. Too much of it fits with the facts that I already know."

"Then you think Mr. Denman really is her husband?"

"I feel positive of it."

"Sure you're not yourself?" he inquired, half humorous, half serious.

"Absolutely sure." My reply was emphatic. "I've never liked the girl."

"I can well understand that." A smile jerked at one corner of his mouth. "It seems to have been mutual," he said dryly.

I could feel my face flushing.

"I beg your pardon," he said kindly. "It pays to be thought priggish by a woman like that. And that was the best thing she could have said to exonerate you. Until then I wasn't sure whether it was the name or the person she was confusing."

In stunned silence I let his words sink in. A mistake of that sort would have made a mess.

"A very abnormal case. She's had a shock of some

sort. But it's hard to know how much of her present condition is due to the blow or to previous anxiety. If there is any truth in her words, Mr. Denman is little less than a cad — and perhaps a murderer," he added in a lower tone.

"Yes, perhaps a murderer," I agreed, and my flesh fairly crept as I recalled how blithely Carla had gone off with him for the afternoon. "But if he is guilty the cause is not that suggested by Bertha Chase."

"No, I should think not," Dr. Whitaker agreed. "Though it seems clear that if he had killed in a fit of jealous rage, it would not have displeased his wife."

We sat silent for a few moments, both of us shocked by the depths of horror Bertha Chase's words had revealed. Finally Dr. Whitaker sighed deeply. "Well, we must reserve our judgment. The girl had evidently suffered to the point of derangement before that blow ever fell. By the way, have you any idea who hit her?"

I had already wondered that, and a suspicion had been born in my mind. She had said she recognized Mark's step and she had interpreted his presence as a protection. What if, instead, it had been he who had struck the blow? Infatuated by Carla he would be only too glad to be rid of Bertha Chase. But there had been a second figure. I must not forget that.

I shook my head slowly. "There are unexplained mysteries about it all," I said.

"I've already told President Mittoff that I suspect Miss Chase's condition to be the result of a

blow, not of an accident. He stopped in this afternoon to see me."

I was glad to hear this piece of information. Now
the president might not regard me wholly as a suspicious, braying ass.

"Of course now I shall have to send for Mr. Denman," Dr. Whitaker continued. "In the light of
what Miss Chase has said, that will be necessary."

"He must never know that she mistook me for
him," I said vehemently.

"Certainly not. I shall merely tell him that in her
delirium she called for him and revealed the fact
of their marriage. And I shall not leave them alone
together," he added half to himself.

"Get in touch with me if there are any new devel-
opments, will you?" I asked at the door. "And — er
— would mind acquainting Miss Johnson and Miss
Manning with the fact that it is Mark Denman, not
I, who is her husband?"

"I shall take pleasure in aiding you to the truth,"
he said kindly. "Goodnight."

I do not know just when it was that I realized
I was being followed. As I left the hospital, my
thoughts were all with my dead friend, Don Crawford. How could I ever have thought him capable of
a secret marriage, and especially of one with Bertha
Chase? I bitterly regretted every doubt of him that
had crossed my mind during the past few days. Suspicion was making a fool of me. Then I thought of
Carla. Of what did I suspect her? Ghastly doubts of
every kind had assailed me recently. I saw now that

they were not the result of ratiocination or of conviction, but of jealousy. I was, in reality, no better than Bertha Chase. Carla had asked me to meet her in her office at nine, and in my pride I had resolved not to do so. It was past that hour now, but I hoped she would be waiting for me.

It was perhaps at that moment, as I turned off Maple Street, that I was fully conscious of stealthy footsteps behind me. Subconsciously I knew that I had heard them before then but had regarded them without suspicion, merely as the ordinary footsteps of any pedestrian on a village street at night. But there was something about the perfect coördination of the steps with mine that made my senses suddenly alert. I walked a bit faster. The footfalls behind me increased in tempo. In the dark shadow of an elm I darted quickly behind the tree trunk. No one approached. My action had been observed.

Apparently I was not to be accosted. It was my destination that my follower wished to know. To go to the library now was out of the question. If danger stalked behind me, I could not bring it to Carla. I decided to go home. It would be a simple matter to slip out a few minutes later. Surely no one would watch the house all night. I walked rapidly up College Avenue, conscious always of those other footsteps that did not advance, that did not lag. At the gate I hesitated a moment. Then I clicked it loudly behind me. In the shade of a lilac bush I waited. No one passed. I counted one hundred slowly. Then I went into the house.

A glance at my watch showed me that it was already ten o'clock. An hour later than the time Carla had specified. Would she wait for me? I doubted it.

There was a light in the front parlor. Miss MacIntyre sat there peacefully reading her Bible. She called to me gently as I passed. "You've had two visitors," she said, "a student who said his name was Morris, and President Mittoff. They wouldn't say what they wanted. But they both insisted on going to your room. Perhaps you'll find some message there."

I thanked her, wondering greatly why it should have been necessary for them to invade my room.

"And Dr. Tyndale?" I asked. "How is he? Have you had any more alarms?"

"No, none. He's been in all afternoon, and this evening he went to bed early. I've been so relieved."

"That's good." I felt relieved myself. I had small desire to be sent off on another wild goose chase after him.

In my room with the lights on, I drew the curtains. In case the person who had followed me were still loitering about I wished to give the impression of retiring, though I had little thought of going to bed. On my desk I found messages from my two callers. Both were scrawled on my memorandum pad.

The first read:

"Had hoped to find you in. Please be so kind as to stop in my office a few moments to-morrow morning before the commencement exercises.

D. K. Mittoff."

The other gave equally small indication of its author's purpose. It merely said:

"I've got a swell idea.
                    B. M."

There was little enough to indicate secrecy. Why either of my two callers should not have intrusted his message to Miss MacIntyre I could not understand. As I stood looking down at the memorandum pad, I saw that there was something different, something changed about my desk. What was it? Then my eyes caught the difference. The center drawer protruded the merest fraction of an inch. And I was positive that I had left it locked. Ever since my discovery of Bertha Chase's letter and of the two sets of gold links, I had been particularly careful never to leave the drawer unlocked. Now I pulled it open hastily. Nothing seemed disturbed. I took out the bundle of letters, into the middle of which I had placed an envelope containing my slender clues. I shook the contents out onto my desk. Yes, there was the letter; there was one pair of gold links. I shook the envelope again. Nothing else fell out. The unidentified gold links were missing.

CHAPTER XVIII

A STRANGE thrill ran through me. During my absence two persons were known to have entered my room. And a clue, which suddenly assumed supreme importance, had been removed. Which of my callers could have taken it? To suspect President Mittoff was out of the question — and yet — and yet it was he who had opposed the presence of a detective. For the first time I recalled the length of time it had taken Dr. Tyndale to fetch him from the reviewing stand the morning Don Crawford's body had been found. What might that signify? They had been as long in arriving as Mark Denman had been, and he had driven out to Mr. Peppersniff's farm to get the coroner. And Benjamin Morris — the story he had told had been verified in every respect by the accounts of others. But were there other things the boy had refrained from mentioning?

Only one fact stood out clearly. My activities were becoming dangerous to some one. The gold links were missing. A figure had followed me on the shadowy streets. Was I nearer the solution of the mystery than I myself suspected? If so, caution must direct my future steps.

And Carla! It was imperative now that I learn her whereabouts. I had already wasted too much time. Had she returned to the library? One person had already been killed there. Another had suffered concussion. What madness had made her suggest that spot as a rendezvous? I saw now, all too clearly, that I should have gone there immediately upon my departure from the hospital. Already I was an hour and a half late for the appointment.

During the time that these thoughts assailed me I had been hastily changing from my Palm Beach into darker clothing. Tan sneakers, blue trousers and a light weight dark sweater completed my costume. I snapped off my light and raised the shades. Best not to tempt the fates by going boldly out the front door, I thought. A giant beech tree raised tortuous branches outside my east window. It would serve perfectly. To remove the screen was the work of but a moment. I dangled for a moment in mid-air. Then I found a foothold. The tree seemed grown for my purpose. In a second I was on the ground.

Here again caution directed my course. Pressing close to the wall of the house, I made my way through the shadows. I crossed the lawn and garden and reached the alley. Which way now? A new idea guided me. Perhaps, after all, Carla was safe. Surely she would not remain in the library after ten o'clock when, as our last night's experience had taught us only too well, the lights were promptly extinguished. It would take only ten minutes at the most to make the detour to her house. I chose the alley route. In

Kingsley the alleys are really grass-grown lanes. I felt no fear of stumbling over ash- or garbage-cans.

Slightly out of breath I trotted down the lane beside her house. A car was drawing up in front. I stood in the deep shadows of the trees, waiting. I thought my last breath was leaving me as I heard Carla's low laughter. Relief poured over me until I swayed. Mark Denman was holding the door of the car open. He walked up the path with her to the door. I could hear her voice plainly.

"I've had a most interesting time."

"Not half so delightful as I have had, and only one of many, I hope." He was holding her hand rather longer than necessary, it seemed to me.

The door closed behind her, the porch light died, and Mark Denman chugged away in his car. I waited a moment, hoping to see the light go on in her room. But the house remained dark. Presently the front door opened again slowly. Carla was on the porch. I whispered her name softly, creeping nearer. I could see the shadow that I knew was hers start nervously.

"Carla," I said again, "it's Tom."

"Tom?" she said incredulously. "Oh, I'm so glad. I was afraid it was some one else."

She came across the grass to me. "I've been so worried. I couldn't get rid of Mark Denman. Did you go to the library?"

"No, I was detained. I've been awfully anxious about you. Why did you ever suggest the library?"

She seemed to recollect something suddenly. "Oh, we must go there now. We must hurry."

I took her arm. "Carla, are you mad? If you have something to tell me, say it here."

She looked at me calmly, her eyes luminous in the shadows. "Are you looking for a small book?" she asked. "An 1805 edition of 'The King and Queen of Hearts' by Charles Lamb?"

I gasped. "Yes, yes I am, but what can you know about it?"

"I know where it is," she replied quietly.

I was too stunned to move. "You know where it is! How — when —"

She interrupted my stammering amazement. "Never mind all that now. I have a feeling that we must hurry, if you want to find it."

She pulled her dark coat closer over her light dress. Silently we hurried across the shadowy campus. Near the chemistry building I saw a light moving. "Be careful," I cautioned. "We don't want to run into the night watchman."

The light moved around the building. "I have my key," whispered Carla. "Is it dark enough for us to slip in the east entrance?"

The shadows lay thick around that corner of the building. I glanced about hastily. So far as I could see we were alone on the quiet campus.

"Quick now," I breathed. In a second the door was open; we were inside. As I turned to make sure that the latch had caught behind us, I thought I saw a shadow moving quickly around the corner. Was it nerves, I asked myself, or had we been followed in spite of our precautions?

"We must hurry," I said. A quick fear for Carla's safety shook me. "Don't use your flash."

Hand in hand we mounted the stairs. I felt by now that every nook and corner of the building was as familiar to my feet as to my eyes. Try as we might to go quietly, the sound of our footsteps set up eerie echoes in the vast silence. That shadow that I had seemed to see moving past the corner of the library! Where was it going? I remembered with dismay the unlocked windows in the basement stacks.

Blindly we felt our way toward the general office. "In here," breathed Carla. With sure step she moved to a case at the front of the room. She stooped and felt along the baseboard. "The key to the case of unexpurgated books," she whispered. She pressed the cold metal into my hand.

Carefully I felt for the lock and turned it.

"The seventh book from the end," she whispered. I heard her counting. Then she pulled out a volume, leafed through it hastily, thrust into my hand a small booklet, and replaced the large book on the shelves. I could hear her breathing rapidly beside me. For all her calm efficiency she, too, felt the menace in the dark solitude.

"Quick," I said again. "We must get out of here." Hastily I locked the case, and she returned the key to its hidden hook.

But we were not quick enough. From the front of the building came the sound of the heavy main door swinging slowly on its hinges. Some one was entering. We could never make our escape without detection,

for we had the length of the room to traverse before
we could reach the wide back corridor. To our right
another doorway gave onto the rotunda. If a light
were flashed from the front entrance where the door
was now swinging open, it would catch us in flight.
We were trapped. Carla's fingers were like ice in my
own.

A sudden hope gleamed in my mind. If my memory of directions were sure, if we did not stumble
over something, we might yet be unobserved. Even
as I thought, I was tiptoeing forward. I stooped, pulling Carla down beside me. Yes, this was the cave-
like counter where I had hidden once before to-day.
The side slid noiselesly back. I pushed Carla into the
opening and followed her. We were none too soon.
Before I had time to shove the slide to, a great circle
of light played over the room. But it came from the
other side of the counter, diminishing as it advanced.
Before the intruder had rounded the counter, we were
shut into its interior together with the dust and spiders. Shut in together! In spite of my alarm I was
conscious of a thrill of joy, for my arm encircled Carla
and our positions were too cramped to allow of any
movement.

I had one eye pressed against the tiny slit left by
the sliding door of our hiding place. Through the
opening I could see the figure of a man make its silent
way to the exact spot where Carla and I had stood
only a moment before. His light flashed on the low
hook. The key was in his hand. The door to the
shelves swung outward. I heard a low exclamation as

he pulled the seventh book from its place. He had known immediately that it had been tampered with. Carla must have replaced it upside down. I felt in my pocket where the small booklet lay. Five minutes more and we would have been too late. The figure by the shelves now seemed to lose all reason. Frenziedly he leafed through all the books on the shelf. I could see the books shake in his grasp. He was evidently holding the light pressed under one arm to allow his hands free play. An awkward movement dislodged it. As it fell to the floor the light flashed off, but not before it had cast a gleam upward into his face. The angry distorted countenance was that of Mark Denman. He looked like a man capable of murder. I could hear him swearing softly to himself as he felt around on the floor for his light. Soon the words became more vehement. The faint click as he pressed the button on his light brought no answering illumination.

It was a trivial accident, but it probably saved us from discovery. Had Mark Denman's light been in order the succeeding events might have had a very different outcome. Suddenly in the midst of a powerful curse the man's voice broke off. The cause was immediately apparent. Far away in the stacks a book had fallen with a loud, hollow boom. Mark Denman took a few cautious steps. About us the silence was so deep that I could hear his breathing. He was standing close beside the large counter where we were hiding. I wondered that he did not hear our own carefully controlled exhalations.

Suddenly he began to move quickly. I heard him knock against a chair. Then he was out of the room. For a moment I could not tell what direction he had taken. Then from the region of the stacks came bang after bang. It sounded like the resurrection day of the classics. Book after book crashed to the floor. A maniac must be loose there.

"Carla, we must get out the front door," I whispered. "Run for it. It's our only chance."

Hastily we crawled from our hiding place and felt our way into the rotunda. In another second we were at the door; then we were outside and it had locked behind us. But our next move was not so easy. I had forgotten that the light over the front entrance remained on all night. I pulled Carla back into the shadow of one of the pillars. We would not be safe here long, I felt. I must get Carla away from that nameless terror that struck down its victims so surely, so quickly.

From our vantage point we commanded a large view of the campus. The shadows lay thick out there on the grass. Anything might lurk there. But anything was preferable to remaining near the building where death walked inscrutable in its purpose. There were ten steps between us and the walk, only ten steps, but they were brightly lighted. At the sides of them, however, abutted low walls of masonry. Perhaps, crouched beside them, we might descend unnoticed. I suggested this plan to Carla and slowly we began our crawling descent.

We were about halfway down when I saw the first shadow. It moved noiselessly beneath a great tree, then leaped suddenly into a ray of light cast by the illumination over the doorway. I was relieved but angry to identify it as Emil Schlachtman's great Dane. What business had the man to let that fearful beast prowl over the campus at night? Its presence there was an open mockery of my warning. Beside it toddled the little Scotty. There was something obscurely repellent in the gigantism of the great Dane as opposed to the nanism of Napoleon, something suggestive that eluded definition. They disappeared again into the shadow.

But now we heard the steady flap flap of the night watchman's feet. Would he ascend the steps and discover us? I felt a momentary regret that we had not walked boldly down in the light. But the steps passed on. He did not so much as flash the light in our direction. We heard him round the corner. In another moment we were down the steps and hurrying in the direction of Campus Avenue.

But before we had left the university grounds I was aware again that we were not alone. Some sixth sense warned me. A movement that might have been caused by a branch, a shadow that was blacker than the other shadows, told me that we were being followed. That Carla realized it too I knew by the half-backward turn of her head. The Music Hall loomed before us.

"Here," I said, and I darted quickly around it.

"We're not going home, after all. We're in danger, but I know where we'll be safe. Take my hand and run for all you're worth."

So it was that, hot and breathless, we turned finally into the walk leading to the infirmary. We had shaken off our pursuer. I rang the bell furiously. Lights flashed on, and then Miss Johnson opened the door.

"Turn off the lights," I commanded her. "Can you put us up for the night?"

"Are you both ill?" she asked, imagining, I suppose, that some dire epidemic was about to break out in the faculty circles at a time of year when she might naturally expect a little rest.

"No, but —" I hardly knew how to explain our predicament, although I felt instinctively that neither of us was safe in his own house that night. Our pursuer knew or guessed too much. Carla's windows opened onto a porch roof, easily accessible to an agile climber. And the beech tree outside my room I knew to be a perfect ladder.

"You see," said Carla artlessly, "we don't want to be brought in on stretchers in the morning."

This remark did little to alleviate the puzzled expression of Miss Johnson's eyes. I hoped that Dr. Whitaker had remembered to tell both nurses that I was not the husband of Bertha Chase.

"I think I'd better call the doctor," I said abruptly. "He'll understand and tell you that it's quite all right for us to be here."

This solution seemed to satisfy the nurse. And after I had talked for a moment with Dr. Whitaker I turned the phone over to Miss Johnson.

With the responsibility removed from her shoulders, she was graciousness itself in showing us to rooms in the same corridor with the one occupied by Bertha Chase.

"Don't go to bed yet, Miss Johnson," I requested. "I want to talk to you for a few moments presently."

"I shall be on night duty until five," she said primly as I stood in the open doorway of Carla's room. Her skirts whispered of starchy virtue as she walked down the corridor.

"A very compromising situation in her eyes," said Carla.

"In mine, too," I said. "I shall expect you to make an honest man of me after this night's adventures."

"Don't be silly." Carla smiled unwillingly. "And run along now. I'm going to sleep."

"You must tell me something first. How did you know where that little booklet was hidden?"

"Mark Denman showed it to me. From hints that he dropped I suspected that he knew something, and I devoted the day to finding out what it was."

Her eyes darkened. "It was rather hard, and it took a bit longer than I had anticipated."

"Carla, are you fond of him?" I knew I had no right to ask the question, but my troubled thoughts spoke before I could restrain them.

Her reply came quickly. "I hate him."

I was surprised at the vehemence of her tone — surprised and shaken with relief.

"Did you know that he was married?"

"Married!" There was an unfathomable horror in her voice.

"Yes, to Bertha Chase."

"Oh, how terrible! So that was his obligation." She sat down suddenly on the bed.

"What do you mean? What obligation are you talking about?"

"He told me he had an obligation to pay off. He was planning to sell that booklet. After that he said he would be free to — " She broke off.

The inference was sufficiently plain. What a day she must have had with him, and how successfully she had played her hand!

"I didn't dream it was anything like that," she said slowly. "So that's why Bertha Chase said she hated me. Oh, the poor girl!"

"Don't pity her too much. She's none too ethical herself. But tell me, did Mark Denman say how he obtained such a valuable book?" I put my hand in my pocket, caressing those few pages. I had not examined the pamphlet yet, but I felt no doubt that it was the one Don Crawford's pencilled notes had referred to.

"He said it had just fallen into his hands. And he laughed too. 'Quite literally it fell into my hands,' he said."

"I wonder what he meant by that. He wasn't just talking nonsense. But it wasn't quite so easy. He did something to make it fall into his hands."

"What do you mean?"

"I hardly know myself."

"I'm glad you were there on the lawn to-night," she said somewhat irrelevantly.

"Why? You weren't going back to the library alone, were you?"

"Why not? I told you to meet me there, didn't I? You might have been waiting. And anyway I'd made up my mind to get that book."

I felt suddenly very humble. I had suspected her of working against me, of being flattered by Mark Denman's attentions, and all the time she had been sure in her purpose, brave in the face of danger. She looked tired and white huddled there on the edge of the bed. I had no words to tell her of my humility. I lifted one of her limp hands and kissed it. "Good-night," I said. "Call if you need me. I shan't go to sleep to-night."

Miss Johnson was sitting very stiff and erect at the desk in Dr. Whitaker's office. "You've got a job on your hands," I told her. "You've got to keep me from falling asleep to-night. And it will be some job, too. I'm dead for sleep."

She gave me a quizzical look. "I have my regular duties. I can't devote the entire night to you. And I don't care for mysteries anyway."

"I shall sit outside Miss Robinson's door," I said emphasizing each word. "And if you admit one other person to this hospital to-night, or if you let me so much as nod, it may well cost you your position." To speak commandingly with no real authority to do so was a very pleasing sensation, I found. "Miss Robinson has been in great danger. There is no necessity for a repetition of the experience."

Miss Johnson was impressed. She unbent with remarkable speed. "I had no idea it was so important," she said apologetically. "You may rely on me."

"Take a look at me every half hour," I said.

I carried the most uncomfortable-looking chair I could see down the corridor and placed it gently outside Carla's door. Then I prepared for several hours of misery, thankful that it was nearly midnight.

For a time I had no difficulty in keeping my eyes open. I had been aching to examine that small book ever since Carla had pressed it into my hand there in the library. Now I removed it carefully from my pocket. The light in the corridor was dim, but bright enough to show me the faded blue wrapper on the book. It was just as the catalogue had described it. I felt a strange thrill run through me. Under the wrapper was a small book. I read the words:

THE

KING AND QUEEN

OF

HEARTS:

WITH THE ROGUERIES OF THE

KNAVE

WHO STOLE AWAY THE QUEEN'S PIES.

ILLUSTRATED IN

FIFTEEN ELEGANT ENGRAVINGS

————

LONDON:

Printed for THOMAS HODGKINS, at the Juvenile Library, Hanway Street (opposite Soho Square), Oxford Street; and to be had of all Booksellers.

————

1805

I paged through it rapidly — a charming pamphlet designed for the pleasure of children, become through its rarity extremely valuable, and, by the merest chance, entangling the lives of grown men and women into a confused net of murder. It lay, light as a feather in my hand, but through its possession Don Crawford now lay with an inescapable weight of earth upon his lifeless body.

I heard a subdued step in the corridor and dropped the booklet hastily into my pocket. Miss Johnson made her conscientious appearance. Without a word she handed me a steaming cup of black coffee. Refreshed and alert I continued my vigil.

From time to time during the silent hours she returned. It must have been three o'clock when I felt a sharp nip on my arm. Miss Johnson stood over me. "You were nodding," she said severely. Then she left, only to return a moment later with another chair. "I'll sit right here ready to pinch you," she said with a wintry smile. Several times thereafter I felt her efficiency. And there we remained together, undisturbed in our odd companionship until six o'clock when I knocked on Carla's door and heard her sleepy voice answer me.

CHAPTER XIX

THOUGH I may have nodded several times during that uncomfortable night, my mind had not been entirely inactive. Indeed, spurred on by fear of Carla's safety, I gave myself up at times to furious thinking. As a result of this mental effort I evolved several theories. Not all of them could be correct. Perhaps none was. But I was certain of one thing. I was dealing with a desperate person. Whether he was immensely clever or I immensely stupid I could not determine. Or perhaps I was simply loath to admit it.

But I had now one distinct advantage. The pamphlet which, in some way, was the root of all the trouble, was in my possession. That fact was due more to Carla's cunning than to my own machinations. How brave and loyal she had been! I hoped she would never discover how many doubts of her integrity I had harbored. Without the pamphlet I should have been completely baffled. But with it in my pocket I formed a plan. I would use it as bait to lure the guilty person into a trap. And there would be witnesses aplenty.

As we thanked Miss Johnson and left the hospital,

I was filled with an intense excitement. The man
hunt was on in earnest. Before another day dawned
I hoped to solve the mystery.

Outside the hospital Carla and I separated, she going off in one direction, I in another. In a town like
Kingsley, whose inhabitants are vitally interested in
the activities of all their neighbors, it pays to be
careful. A little thing like murder can escape attention, but let me be seen escorting Carla home before
the breakfast hour and all the tongues in the village
would wag.

Sheltered by its beautiful old trees, Miss MacIntyre's house slumbered peacefully in the early morning light. Dew still glistened on the grass and flowers.
An impalpable veil of loveliness seemed wrapped
about the place. I stood at the gate for a moment fill-
ing my eyes with the beauty. The events of last night
seemed incongruous. Had I really climbed down that
sturdy beech tree? A glance at the unscreened window assured me that I had. I should doubtless have
to do a little murdering on my own account now. My
room must harbor some dozens of flies. But they
would have an hour or two more of activity, I
thought, as I let myself quietly into the cool hallway. I would not disturb the two elderly inhabitants
of the house by whacking the life out of a few
insects.

But it took far less noise than that, I discovered
a moment later, to rouse Miss MacIntyre. As I shut
the door gently behind me, I was conscious of a faint
rustling in the front parlor. Miss MacIntyre came

quickly to the doorway. Her sweet old face looked pinched and tired.

"Oh, Mr. Allen," she said tremulously, "have you found him?"

"Found whom?" I tried to keep my voice low, but her appearance and words had startled me.

"Dr Tyndale. He's been gone all night." Her old voice quavered.

"Been gone all night! Are you sure? How do you know?"

"That woman," she said. "She telephoned here at midnight for him. I knocked at his door, and when I couldn't rouse him I went in. His bed was empty. He hadn't been in it, and he was gone. I went to summon you, and your room was empty, too. I thought, of course, you'd gone to protect him as you promised to do." Tears stood in her reproachful eyes.

"No," I replied. "No, I wasn't with him." I wished I could comfort her. Her delicate hands trembled against the door frame. She looked as if she might fall. I lowered my eyes from her distressed face, and what I saw made me catch my breath. Her white shoes were dusty and grass-stained.

"And did you sit up all night?" I asked as calmly as possible.

"Yes, I came downstairs and sat in the front parlor all night." Her eyes looked pitiful and beseeching.

Simultaneously two thoughts struck me with stunning import. One was the realization that I had only the word of Miss MacIntyre that Dr. Tyndale was

being threatened. The other was the memory that
Don Crawford had once lived in this house. He had
told me of it when I had moved in, and I had never
thought of it again. "A beautiful house," he had
said. "I hope you'll get along there better than I
did. I lived there four months once and left under
rather unpleasant circumstances." That was all. But
why had I not remembered it sooner? The unpleasant circumstances that he had spoken of could not,
however, have been very serious, for often on his
way to my room he had stopped in for a friendly word
of greeting with Dr. Tyndale. Miss MacIntyre's
manner with him had always been a trifle stiff, but
so had it been with me until she had unburdened her
fears to me yesterday.

My thoughts had carried me away from Miss Mac-
Intyre and up the stairs. Dr. Tyndale's closed door
halted me. Gently I turned the handle and looked
into the large book-lined room. A great four-poster
stood in one corner. On one of its pillows rested Dr.
Tyndale's gray head. He lay quietly, not rousing
at my entrance, and as I looked at him I saw the
covers rise and fall with his even breathing. I had
never before seen him without his spectacles. Sleep
robbed him of much of his intellectual expression. He
looked simply like a tired old man. Could it be true
that this harmless old soul was in danger? I closed
the door softly.

"Dr. Tyndale is in bed asleep," I said a bit sharply
to Miss MacIntyre waiting anxiously at the foot of
the stairs. "You were evidently mistaken."

"But he was not there," she protested.

"Probably he was taking a bath," I said bluntly, and I proceeded to my room before I had time to see a flush dye those fastidious features.

My own bed looked remarkably inviting, and, setting my alarm for eight-thirty, I snatched an hour of sleep. That gave me just time for a cold bath and a bite at George and Harry's. The academic procession was to form at ten in front of the library. At fifteen minutes before the hour I announced myself to Dr. Mittoff's secretary and was ushered into his office.

"I haven't much time now, Allen," he said, "but I wanted you to know that I'm putting a detective on the case to-morrow. I've had a talk with Dr. Whitaker, and I think that, despite the notoriety which may result, but which we shall do our best to suppress, that course is necessary."

"But — " I began. My remark, however, was cut short.

"You've done your best, I'm sure, Allen. But it has come to my attention that this affair is more serious than I at first imagined.

He paused a second, and I seized the opportunity. "By to-morrow, sir," I said confidently, "the affair will be settled."

He looked at me keenly. "What's that? You know who the criminal is?"

"Not yet," I replied. "But I'm going to try a little experiment. I'd like you to be present. In the rotunda of the library at four this afternoon."

"I shall be there without fail," he replied firmly, and I thought I detected the merest fragment of a smile at the corners of his mouth.

We shook hands and I took my departure, struggling into my gown and hood as I hurried across the campus.

There is something both ludicrous and impressive about an academic procession. The instructors, those newcomers to the profession of teaching, look embarrassed and self-conscious in their unadorned, funereal A.B. robes of cotton or poplin. The full professors find on such an occasion some compensation for their years of toil on starvation salaries. They carry themselves with pride, wearing with dignity their silken robes bedight with the colors of their department. They switch their hoods like gaily colored tails, and they gaze cross-eyed past the golden tassels dangling from the left of their caps. Between these two extremes of embarrassment and pride march the assistant and associate professors gazing scornfully about them, cracking quiet jokes about their accomplices in education.

For a full half hour while the marshal, with due regard for degree and length of servitude, whipped into line the three hundred members of the staff, I had opportunity to gaze about at the mediæval spectacle. Carla, I was pleased to note, retained her charm even when swathed in a black robe and capped by the ridiculous mortar board which custom has long decreed. Mark Denman hovered near her, his dark eyes flashing his admiration. Did he, I wondered, connect her with the disappearance of the booklet from his office? And what had caused the dark bruise on his right cheek bone? I would have given a good deal to know what had gone on there in the stacks after our departure.

Now, I decided, was the best time to take the initial step in my plan. I approached Carla and Mark Denman first.

"I wonder if you could both step into the library at four this afternoon," I said. "I've just discovered a book among Don Crawford's possessions that he wanted left to the library. It's fairly valuable. I thought you both might be interested in seeing it — you especially, Denman, since you're the librarian here."

Carla gave me a frightened look. Mark Denman's eyes narrowed. His mouth straightened into a thin line.

"Thank you," he said. "It sounds most interesting. I'll not forget to be on hand."

"And you?" I turned to Carla.

"Yes, thank you. I'm free this afternoon."

I turned abruptly and approached Dr. Tyndale, who was fussing over the arrangement of his hood.

"Let me lend a hand," I said. I fastened the elastic tab onto the back of his gown. "If you're not busy this afternoon," I said, "I wish you'd come over to the library at four. Don Crawford left a fairly valuable book to the University, and I'm going to give it to the president at that time. I thought you might like to be present."

He peered at me through his thick glasses. "Dear me, dear me," he murmured. "That is interesting. A gift to the University. Well, one man's loss is another man's gain, as they say."

I drew away, slightly repelled by his callousness. He leaned toward me apologetically. "Hardly the right thing to say under the circumstances though, is it? Well, it's good of you to think of me. I'll try to be there. At four-thirty, you say?"

"At four," I replied firmly.

I turned away. "At four, at four," I heard him muttering absent-mindedly to himself.

I walked away toward the rows of Seniors. They were already in formation, lined up in alphabetical order. I had no difficulty in finding Benjamin Morris. I repeated my invitation.

"Oh, I say," he broke in. "I was leaving town with the folks at three o'clock."

It was on the tip of my tongue to remark, "The word 'folks' is a provincialism." But I refrained, replying merely with all the superiority I could muster, "Well, I'm afraid you can't go. This is important."

His eyes brightened. "A clue!" he cried excitedly.

I did not answer him. Instead, I asked, "Why were you in my room yesterday? What is that idea of yours?"

He looked a little sheepish. "I thought it was a swell idea yesterday, but probably you'll think it's lousy. I just had an inspiration about that dame with the cane. I remembered that Thursday evening I distinctly heard her cane tapping on the glass floor.

And Saturday night just before I got that wallop, I found marks of a rubber tip all over the floor there. Funny doings, eh wot?"

There was something repugnant to me about the young man's English. He had studied under my direction for three years, too.

"You were in poor condition to judge the sound of anything Thursday evening," I replied coldly. "I shall expect you at the library at four."

He seemed a bit subdued. "Yes, sir, I'll be there even if the folks are disappointed."

I shuddered as I left him.

Aside from Bertha Chase, whose presence at the library would, of course, be out of the question, there remained now uninvited only Agnes Hubbard and Miss MacIntyre. I should count on catching them at noon. I hurried back to my position in the procession, and none too soon. It was already ten-thirty.

Every one was now in place, and we began our long march across the campus. It is a custom at Kingsley to parade about the buildings in our regalia in order that those unfortunates who have not procured tickets to the Commencement exercises may still be privileged to behold us trapped out in our finery. The double line was led by the college marshal. Following him came the Seniors, then the candidates for graduate degrees, pallid souls on the verge of nervous breakdown. After them stalked the faculties of the various colleges, from graduate assistants on up. At the end of the line walked the trustees with President Mittoff and the speaker of the day.

At the doors of University Hall the order was reversed. The couples parted, one to each side, forming a long gantlet through which we were all forced to walk, an old form of punishment turned into a ceremonial rite of distinction. As the inverted procession passed me, and before it came my turn to step into place and follow, I had an opportunity to study those of higher rank passing before me. President Mittoff, handsome and distinguished, carried on a nonchalant but dignified conversation with the Commencement speaker. The dark red bands of his gown looked uncomfortably hot. I was amused to note how his Phi Beta Kappa key appeared to precede him, dangling on a watch chain across his unmistakable pouch. Then, for something to do, I began to count the honor keys as their proud owners filed past.

I saw Dr. Tyndale approach, shuffling a bit as he came, gazing straight before him, tall and unsmiling in his colorful robes. This was no circus parade for him, I knew. He loved the pomp of the occasion, the recognition accorded to learning. The whole bearing of the man bespoke his reverence for the ceremony. His academic robe fell back a bit as he passed me. Another Phi Beta Kappa key!

Soon it was my turn to slip into line. I could no longer pursue my game of counting keys. Setting my face into what I hoped was a properly forbidding expression, I marched between the endless lines of lesser faculty members and students. The long procession moved slowly down the center aisle of the auditorium, between the rows and rows of visitors and townspeople, up onto the platform. The agony of another Commencement morning had begun. I found my place and stood watching those who had followed me mount the platform. It was unimaginably boring, and I was overwhelmingly sleepy. I resumed my game of counting keys.

Suddenly my mind jerked to a new idea. I realized that subconsciously there had been a purpose in my pastime. Or perhaps it was merely a coincidence that now impressed me. Whatever it was, I was tantalized by a fugitive connection of incident. It eluded me for a moment. All I knew was that in Phi Beta Kappa keys lay some significance pertaining to the mysteries of the past few days. For as I had counted the keys flashing by me, I had realized that almost every one of the actors in the drama of the library wore this emblem of scholarship. President Mittoff, Dr. Tyndale, Mark Denman, Carla Robinson, and I myself. Bertha Chase, I remembered, occasionally wore one on a chain around her neck. Agnes Hubbard, too, I recalled, had been awarded one this year. In fact, her credit hours had totalled more than any one else in her class. About Benjamin Morris I was not so sure, and I waited in an inexplicable fever of interest throughout the long prosy speech on "The History of Education in This State." The awarding of degrees began. How long it took to reach the M's. Then the name Morris was called.

The boy advanced across the platform. Yes, there it was — the flashing gold Phi Beta Kappa key.

I sank back relaxed to my chair. What was it all about? What did it matter? It proved nothing, after all. Miss MacIntyre was in the picture too, and I had never known her to wear the emblem. What was I trying to prove? What was the connection?

The answer flashed to my mind so quickly that I almost forgot to rise for the final hymn. I stumbled to my feet, my thoughts whirling. As distinctly as if I were gazing at a picture projected on the screen, I saw a small black Scotty waddling up the walk to Miss MacIntyre's house. I saw its dignified pose as it watched the great Dane lope off down the street, and I saw myself bend to examine something glittering on its collar — a Phi Beta Kappa key. A Phi Beta Kappa key that bore the name Oscar Bartlett. I glanced hastily at the program in my hand. I could not find the name among the members of the graduating class nor among the candidates for a higher degree. He must then be a Junior, for only members of the two upper classes were eligible for the honor. I groaned to myself. If he were a Junior, then he had in all probability left town. Undergraduates usually wasted no time in getting away. I must find the registrar immediately and learn the boy's whereabouts. All my theories were pricked by this new discovery.

After the recessional I found Carla. "Wait for me here, please," I urged. "I won't be a minute."

I caught sight of the registrar making strides toward home and luncheon. I hastened after him. "Mr. Cummings," I called.

He waited, mopping his face as I approached.

"Could you tell me whether there is any one about the college named Bartlett — Oscar Bartlett?"

He puckered his tiny red mouth. "I don't recall the name, but we can soon determine."

We retraced our steps to University Hall where his office was located. He picked up a directory. "No," he said smugly, "no Oscar Bartlett. I thought I was right. The nearest approach to the name is Oswald Barrett, a Freshman."

I was nonplussed. Much as I had disliked the entry of a new factor into the case, I had not anticipated difficulty in discovering the owner of the key. There was, however, another possibility. I recalled that I had not noticed the date on the key. It might belong to an alumnus.

"Do you have a register of the alumni who have been back for commencement?"

It was quickly produced in alphabetized form. Oscar Bartlett's name was not included.

Mr. Cummings was growing restive. I thanked him, and we left, he to hurry home to a sharp-nosed wife and four unattractive children, I to find Carla reading and rereading notices on the bulletin board outside University Hall.

"Are you willing to sacrifice more time to me?" I inquired.

"I'm willing to enjoy some with you," she smiled.

"That's what I mean. No more adventures for a few hours. In fact, we're going to fly from them."

We stopped only to invite Miss MacIntyre and Agnes Hubbard to be present at the library at four. The former accepted rather timidly, the latter with unconcealed eagerness when I told her of the discovery of the valuable object entrusted to her desk.

"What is it?" she wanted to know.

"You'll see this afternoon," I told her. I knew nothing could keep her away.

Then off we sallied in "School's Out" down the elm-shaded streets through which we had dodged the preceding evening, out into the open country, headed for the Tulip Tree Inn.

"Only one question," I said to Carla. "Did you ever hear of an Oscar Bartlett?"

"Never," she responded quickly. "And one question from me, too. Where are you keeping that booklet?"

"Right here," I said patting my vest pocket. "That's one reason we're getting out of town. I have no intention of being hit on the head and robbed, not until four o'clock at any rate."

The possibility that either of these eventualities would occur after that hour did not enter my mind. I was egotistically confident of my scheme.

The subject was not mentioned between us again. That Carla was the most enchanting creature in the world I was ready to swear, as I drew up in front of 711 Campus Avenue at quarter to four.

"Don't delay," I cautioned her.

"I won't. You'll see me in the library on the dot. But do be careful. I don't know quite why, but I have a premonition that something else is going to happen."

"So have I," I told her. "But only that the murderer will betray himself."

She shook her head half doubtfully.

"You'll see," I said, and sped away to remind Miss MacIntyre and Dr. Tyndale of their engagement.

CHAPTER XX

I FOUND them sitting together on the verandah trying with more perseverance than skill to make Napoleon shake hands with them. Dr. Tyndale was chuckling quietly, and half the wrinkles in Miss MacIntyre's face were dispelled by her laughter at the terrier's antics.

Her smiling eyes met mine as I came onto the porch. "You've just had a telephone call, Mr. Allen," she said. "The number's on the pad there in the hall."

"471" I read, recognizing it as the number of the infirmary.

Dr. Whitaker's agitated voice greeted me. "Miss Chase is gone," he said immediately. "She must have slipped out about fifteen minutes ago when the nurses were busy with an emergency case, one of the faculty children. She's been normal all day, but weak. We're doing our best to locate her. Just thought I'd warn you."

After a few more remarks we hung up. I felt obscurely worried at this unexpected development. What new mischief would the girl perpetrate? But

I could do nothing now. A glance at my watch showed me that it was already five minutes to the hour. I joined Miss MacIntyre and Dr. Tyndale on the porch. As we walked together to the library, I noticed that Miss MacIntyre leaned rather heavily on her cane. It tapped with persistent regularity on the cement walks. The little Scotty toddled after us.

The others were all waiting for us, seated around an oak table at the right of the rotunda — Carla, pale and quiet; Agnes Hubbard, obviously excited, with two spots of bright red burning in her cheeks; Mark Denman with a mocking, cynical look on his dark face; Benjamin Morris, nervous and ill at ease; Dr. Mittoff, dignified and aloof as an onlooker at a children's party. I was surprised to see one uninvited guest. Emil Schlachtman, as spick and span as a frayed, much worn suit could make him, stood by the desk, one hand on the collar of his enormous dog. At my entrance he gave me a servile smile.

"It iss a bad dog, all right, Provessor," he said. "I find him in der library efen in day time. Come Obie, dis iss no place for us." He shambled slowly to the door.

A quick suspicion darted into my mind. Obie was a strange name for a dog. O. B. were the initials of Oscar Bartlett. What the connection was I could not see. Probably mere coincidence. But I called to him. "Don't go. Just put your dog out. As night watchman here you may be interested in a gift the library is about to receive, something of a little value."

A veiled look, almost of triumph, came over his face. I saw President Mittoff raise his eyebrows slightly. For a moment I regretted my impulse, regretted, indeed, this entire enterprise. What had I expected to gain by this melodramatic setting? In the troubled hours of last night my wits must have taken leave of me. I had had some wild notion that the person who had been desperate enough to murder Don Crawford would be sufficiently reckless to make one last attempt to obtain possession of the booklet as I passed it around for inspection. I had determined to keep my eye on the booklet, to scrutinize the actions of every person present. To my mind none of them, with the exception of Carla, was above suspicion. But now in the sane light of day with the little group gathered together there in the rotunda, my scheme seemed fantastic in the extreme. No one, of course, would be so foolhardy as to risk the detection of eight pairs of eyes. Nor was I even sure that the murderer was present. Who and where was the mysterious Oscar Bartlett?

While these doubts had been flooding my mind, I had obtained the assistance of Benjamin Morris to move the heavy oak table to the center of the rotunda, where the light shining down from the glass windows of the high dome cast no shadows. Nine chairs were pulled up to the table. Every one was seated. President Mittoff looked amused and skeptical as I began my remarks.

"All of us here," I said, "were shocked a few days ago at the discovery of Don Crawford's death. We are all of us to some extent bound together by this event, some of us because we saw the body lying in the stacks, others because we saw him often as he moved about performing his accustomed tasks in the library.

"You may recall that President Mittoff asked me on Friday to take charge of Don Crawford's affairs. Since that time I have discovered among his possessions a little booklet which, under the circumstances, it seems appropriate to present to the library. It has some value, not a great deal, but its rarity will make it an interesting addition to the old books belonging to Kingsley University. I am, therefore, on behalf of my dead friend, turning it over to President Mittoff."

I pulled from my pocket the tiny book in its blue wrapper and passed it to the president, who sat at one end of the table. In spite of his slightly mocking expression, he looked at it, I noted, with a good deal of interest, examining the cover and pointing out to Dr. Tyndale, who sat at his left on one side of the table, the date 1805. Dr. Tyndale peered at it carefully with his nearsighted eyes, and as he passed it on to Miss MacIntyre they examined together some of the charming old engravings. Miss MacIntyre seemed entranced with the little book. She fingered it lovingly, smiling with almost a child's delight at the quaint rhymes and pictures. Finally she handed it to Carla, whose trembling hands did no more than turn a few pages before she held it out to Emil Schlachtman. Seated at the end of the table facing President Mittoff, the night watchman had seemed an indifferent spectator as the little book had passed from hand to hand. But his interest quickened as his gnarled fingers closed on the pamphlet. He looked at it curiously.

"I know not'ings about old buchs," he said. "It iss strange dot a leetle t'ing like dis could be wort' a lot of money."

He weighed it in his hand a moment, as if estimating its value in poundage. Then he handed it, rather reluctantly it seemed, to Mark Denman seated around the corner of the table to his left. I moved my chair a bit to a position at the end of the table beside President Mittoff. Mark Denman looked at me with raised eyebrows. With his right forefinger he tapped the booklet in his left hand.

"An interesting acquisition," he pronounced narrowing his eyes a trifle. "Very interesting in many respects. Mr. Morris, are you an authority on old books?" His tone was mocking as he passed it to the boy beside him.

"I'm afraid not," Benjamin Morris replied, a nervous laugh following his words. He handled the little book gingerly, as if loath to touch anything once the property of his rival. Odd, I thought, that his jealousy could extend even to the grave. He watched Agnes Hubbard closely as she took the book from his hands.

The girl's excitement was evident. Bright spots

of color burned in her cheeks. Then they faded, leaving her face amazingly pale.

"This is really it," she exclaimed impetuously. "And just to think — "

I was about to interrupt her, fearful lest in her ebullition she betray some previous knowledge of the object. But there came at this moment another interruption, entirely unexpected to us all. The front door of the library had evidently not been securely fastened, for it was flung suddenly open, and Bertha Chase darted toward us. She seemed aware of only one person in our small gathering.

"Darling," she cried, and threw her arms about Mark Denman's neck. "Darling, I've had such terrible dreams. Don't let go of me. Oh, never let go of me again."

I saw Mark Denman struggling to free himself. I heard about me exclamations of astonishment, and I turned to reach across the table to Agnes Hubbard.

"Give me the booklet quick," I told her.

She looked at me, wordless, unmoving.

"I haven't got it," she said finally, her eyes filled with horror.

"But you had it last," I said, looking quickly up and down the bare table. Every one was intent on the tableau at the end. Chairs had been pushed back; President Mittoff and Benjamin Morris were on their feet as if uncertain whether or not to interfere in the struggle which, to them, was inexplicable as well as startling.

I was scarcely aware of Mark Denman's actions.

My own immediate problem was much more vital. In the instant that the door had been flung open I had turned involuntarily in my chair. And in that split second of time the booklet had disappeared. Why had I ever removed my eyes from it? I should have been prepared for any contingency — even this.

The commotion at the end of the table seemed to be lessening. Benjamin Morris had dragged his chair around and Bertha Chase was seated in it, white and shaking and holding fast to Mark Denman's hand. His face was a study in baffled anger, but I had no time to contemplate it. There was not a moment to lose. I took advantage of the moment of silence and rose to my feet, shoving my chair over to Benjamin Morris, who slouched into it.

"I shall ask you all to remain where you are," I said, and my voice echoed loudly in the great rotunda. "This interruption has proved most inopportune. At the moment when Miss Chase, or rather Mrs. Denman, made her entrance, the booklet I was exhibiting disappeared."

There was a murmur around the table, punctuated by a few quickly drawn breaths at my double announcement. Mark Denman looked at me angrily. I saw him dart a quick glance at Carla.

"This is a serious loss," I continued, "more serious probably than the majority of you realize. If the booklet has fallen to the floor, we can find it easily, or if any one in a spirit of fun has slipped it into a pocket, I must advise him to produce it at once. This is not the time for joking."

Immediately feet were lifted, chairs pushed back. I examined the floor quickly. The booklet was not there. I pulled out the table drawers. They were empty. I looked at President Mittoff. His face wore an expression of baffled amazement as he returned my regard.

"You understand, sir, I think, the seriousness of the occasion," I said addressing him. He nodded briefly.

"I need not go into all the details now," I said, letting my eyes rest deliberately and separately on each of the other faces turned to me. "It is, however, a matter of importance that the booklet be found before any of those present leaves the library." My words were followed by a moment of complete silence.

"Miss Hubbard," I continued, "you were the last to have the booklet. Try to remember, if you can, what happened when Mrs. Denman entered. Possibly in the excitement of the moment you dropped it on the table. Can you recall its leaving your fingers?"

The girl lifted frightened eyes to mine. "I know I had it," she said, her breath catching as she spoke. "But when you asked me for it, it was gone. That's all I know."

"Could you have slipped it inside your dress?" I persisted.

Benjamin Morris was on his feet instantly. "Are you insinuating that she tried to steal it?" he demanded hotly.

"I am insinuating nothing," I replied. "Though

if I wished to, I might remind you that you were
sitting next to Miss Hubbard and might easily have
procured the booklet yourself."

"Well, I can tell you I didn't," he replied belliger-
ently. "And what about yourself? You were on the
other side of her."

"True enough," I answered as calmly as possible.

I turned to the others, all leaning forward on the
table with the exception of Bertha Chase, who lay
back in her chair, her eyes closed, apparently indifferent to anything that took place so long as her
hand rested in one of Mark Denman's. "I think
by now that you must all realize that in order to remove suspicion from all but the offending person it is
necessary that we all be searched. But before we
submit to that process, I offer one more chance to
some one to produce the booklet and terminate what
is perhaps a very bad joke."

No one moved. Then Emil Schlachtman began
to turn out his pocket on the table. An odd assort-
ment of dirty handkerchiefs, bolts, flashlight bat-
teries, and bits of paper lay before him. I saw Carla
draw slightly away from him, leaning back in her
chair.

"A very commendable spirit of frankness, I will
admit," I said, gazing at the growing pile of odds
and ends among which I was interested to note
several pencils of the type used in the library. "But
we must be considerably more thorough than that
I am afraid. I propose that one at a time the men
step into the general office with me where I shall

search their clothing and shall myself submit to being searched by any one you may designate. After which Miss Robinson will search the women present and allow herself to be examined by either Miss MacIntyre or Miss Hubbard. Mrs. Denman, I think, after her recent illness is scarcely in condition to be relied upon."

An angry snort from Mark Denman greeted my last remark. It was occasioned, I imagined, less by the reference to the almost recumbent position of Mrs. Denman than to my repeated references to his wife as such. He made, however, no attempt to deny the relationship. He would, no doubt, have made more attempt at a bluff had not President Mittoff been present.

Several remonstrances greeted my announcement. Miss MacIntyre, as might have been expected, was extremely averse to being searched. "I can assure you all," she said with delicate precision, "that I am concealing no booklet in my clothing."

"*Gott sei dank,* my clothes iss clean to der skin," said Emil Schlachtman, leering around the circle and bringing his eyes to light finally on Miss MacIntyre.

She drew herself erect in her chair, looking appealingly at Dr. Tyndale, who seemed almost as unaware of what was going on as was Mrs. Denman.

"But see here," cried Benjamin Morris, "that won't prove anything. Suppose some one planted the book on some one else."

"If you mean — " began Agnes Hubbard, when President Mittoff put a period to the remarks.

"Mr. Morris' suggestion is hardly tenable, I believe," he said gravely. "I propose that we carry out Mr. Allen's suggestion without further ado. I shall offer myself as the first victim."

Together we entered the general office where I made a thorough job of the matter. I should have been inclined to credit Benjamin Morris' suggestion had I discovered the booklet on President Mittoff, but I found nothing incriminating, and he returned to the rotunda to send in Dr. Tyndale. Then one by one all the men of the group submitted to being searched. Dr. Tyndale, rather helpless and absentminded; Mark Denman (who had difficulty in extricating his hand from his wife's clasp), scornful and suspicious; Benjamin Morris, nervous and excited; and finally Emil Schlachtman, obviously proud of his clean linen. Commencement day was evidently a gala occasion for his wardrobe. As I helped him on with his coat, a feeling of baffled despair overcame me. Though I had searched each man as carefully as a custom inspector looking for a diamond, some one, I felt, had proved too clever for me.

President Mittoff was elected to retaliate upon my person. He did so unsparingly.

"Well, Allen, what do you make of it now?" he inquired as I laced up my shoes.

"I've been a fool," I admitted. "I've bungled it."

He did not deny it. "I'll have a detective here in the morning," he promised.

As we stepped back into the rotunda, a beam of light from the high dome windows shot into my eye.

I lowered my head. And as I did so I knew that no detective would be on the campus on the morrow. And I knew that, while I must allow Miss MacIntyre, Mrs. Denman, Agnes Hubbard and Carla herself each to play her part in this game of Hunt the Booklet, no discovery of its presence on any woman here would be made. As Carla searched them one by one, and as each returned, justified in her innocence to the table in the rotunda, I laid my plans. For a chance ray of sunlight had directed my eyes. Caught in the iron work of the immense central chandelier, I had seen the blue-covered booklet.

CHAPTER XXI

W E STOOD, the ten of us, on the steps of the library, the great door locked behind us. Ready to go our separate ways, we lingered a moment, eyes searching eyes, a suspicion and a dread evident in every one present.

I spoke clearly so that all of them should hear, addressing my remarks first to Miss MacIntyre.

"Don't expect me in this evening," I said. "A friend is driving me to the city and we don't expect to get back until early in the morning. As I'm late already, I'll just leave my car in front of the house for the night."

I was conscious that every one was listening attentively to my words, just as I wished them to. There was surprise in Carla's eyes, and a stern speculative expression in President Mittoff's. I turned to him. "May I see you in your office in the morning, sir?" I asked.

"At ten o'clock," he said briefly. I knew he was displeased at my conduct of the affair and at my apparent indifference to it now.

The little group broke up with wary, distrustful

glances at one another. Benjamin Morris approached
me.

"How long do I have to stick around in this
dump?" he inquired.

"Until to-morrow afternoon, at least. I'll get in
touch with you at noon."

"You don't think I know anything about that
booklet, do you?" he asked hotly. Behind him I saw
Agnes Hubbard's face, pale and fearful.

"I'm asking you to stay to help me," I evaded.
"You've given me some good hints so far."

He preened himself at this exaggeration. "Well,"
he admitted, "I think myself that idea about the
tapping of the cane was a pretty good one. Think
it over, will you? There's something funny there,
though I can't figure it out."

I promised to meditate on the matter. Then I
bade them good-bye. As I descended the library
steps I could see that the others were, by now, well
dispersed. Mark Denman was hustling his wife down
the slant walk. President Mittoff was strolling
toward his office. Emil Schlachtman was headed
for the stadium behind which his small house was
located. His great Dane and Dr. Tyndale's Scotty
followed him. Even Carla had gone. I could see
her with Miss MacIntyre and Dr. Tyndale, curbing
her steps to their slow ones. It was just as well, I
thought, that she had not lingered for a word with
me. I had no desire to acquaint her with my real
plans. She would have attempted to dissuade me,
I knew, and I was determined in my purpose.

Now was certainly the strategic moment for carrying out my first step. With the backs of all my late companions turned to me, I walked briskly around the library. At the rear of the building I parted the thick shrubbery, slid up the window, and stepped over the sill. It was foolish to feel as excited as I did, but my heart was beating a staccato tattoo against my ribs. I am by nature a frank man, and the sundry deceits I had practiced during the past few days had somehow unnerved me. I had become apprehensive of the least sound. But as I stood there in the basement stacks, only the buzzing of a fly on a pane of glass greeted my ears. The silence of the immense building was deathlike. Deathlike too, in the dim light were the rows and rows of books neatly arranged in their steel sarcophagi.

I moved quietly over the glass floors and up the steel staircases until I had reached the main floor. I pushed open the door into the rotunda, rounded the semicircular desk and stood again looking up at the chandelier. Yes, there was the blue-wrappered booklet lodged in the iron grille work just as I had seen it when that accidental beam of light directed my eyes to it. I felt the muscles of my throat tighten. I had no intention of removing the booklet. Its possession alone meant nothing. But to see it in the hand of some one who, I was confident, would return for it, meant revenge and retribution for the death of my friend. I smiled to myself. The trap was set, and far more skillfully than I had planned. Now only the culprit and I knew where the booklet was hidden.

I had only to wait, but to wait in such a place

as to be completely hidden. I must see and yet be, myself, unseen. As I gazed about the rotunda I saw the impossibility of using it as a hiding place. In fact, I had chosen it for my afternoon's experiment because of this very reason. It was vast and bare. I saw how unerringly the culprit had chosen the only available spot where an object might be undiscovered. What a chance he had taken! In the one moment when all eyes were directed toward the front door, he had tossed the booklet up into the chandelier. What an unerring aim! And the probability that it would not lodge there had been tremendous. But luck had been with him so far.

As I prowled around, looking in vain for a hiding place, I came to the clear glass doors of the general office. Here was a possibility. I had twice before remained undiscovered in this room. Perhaps I could do so a third time. The counter I had previously employed was out of the question, being too far removed from the doorway to give a view of the rotunda. But there were other counters. Two of them extended inward at right angles to the door. The one to the left would furnish an advantageous view of the central portion of the rotunda. To my joy I found that it also was fitted up with a sliding door. But the interior was filled with books, pamphlets, and cards. It would be necessary to remove them. I did so cautiously, stopping now and then to cock an ear for the slightest noise, any cracking or tapping that might indicate I was not alone. It was a lengthy business, for the only vacant spot I

could discover was the dusty counter at the end
of the room where Carla and I had hidden the previous evening. But at last the removal was accomplished, and I discovered, pleasurably enough, that
my new hiding place was comparatively clean and
at least free of spiders.

But now one more obstacle presented itself. The
sliding door creaked dolefully. I hunted about until
I had located a small oil can. A few applications
worked wonders. Now I could crawl into my hole
and shove the door back and forth without fear of
detection. Had I known how long my wait was to
be I should not have been so eager to dispose myself
in the musty, uncomfortable tomb I had prepared. I
felt conspicuous even to myself; so I arranged my
frame as comfortably as possible and resolved to
endure it.

And now my thoughts, long held in abeyance, set
up a chatter and gossip that I could no longer avoid.
I tried to marshal them into order, but they skipped
around to please themselves while I endeavored to
grasp a tail of one of them and simply hang on. The
first tail I took hold of was the long snaky one of the
dog, Obie. The fancy that had flashed to mind
earlier in the afternoon returned. Could there be any
connection in that name and in the initials of Oscar
Bartlett? It was a long chance, but I was convinced
that there were dark and hidden mysteries that
would not clear themselves until my hand was
actually upon the murderer. It was a strange coincidence that had fastened on Napoleon, the con-

stant companion of Obie, a Phi Beta Kappa key
bearing the name Oscar Bartlett. And what had become of the key? Had Dr. Tyndale or Miss MacIntyre removed it? If so I had heard no mention of the
fact, and a circumstance as humorous as that would
naturally be commented upon. But who was Oscar
Bartlett, and who had placed his key on the collar of
the little dog? Instantly there flashed to my mind
the one person who, doubtless, saw with more fre-
quency than any one else the squat form of the
terrier waddling about the campus. Emil Schlachtman! But where would he obtain the key, granted
the opportunity to fasten it on Napoleon? A sudden idea startled me to a more erect position and
sent my head banging on the top of the counter.
Perhaps Emil Schlachtman was Oscar Bartlett! The
idea seemed preposterous, but I could not let go
of it. And then another thought impinged itself on
my consciousness. The key bearing Oscar Bartlett's
name had been fastened to the little dog's collar with
a gold chain. Why had I not thought of that before?
Now I could not for the life of me recall the size of
the links. Could they have matched the two I had
found by Don Crawford's body? I had no means of
knowing. Both the chain and the links had vanished.

Or perhaps the key had been the property of Miss
MacIntyre, left to her by some long-dead relative,
or better still by a long-lost lover. What memories
had stirred in her eyes as she recalled those youth-
ful occasions when she had crawled through a base-

ment window? Perhaps her account of her Thursday evening activities had not been so accurate as she had led me to believe. As far as that went, not one of the persons I had suspected had an alibi for the hour of the crime — from eight to nine. Carla and Mark Denman had been together from eight-thirty on, but what had they been doing before then? Carla had been in her office, she said, and now, thank Heaven, I no longer distrusted her slightest word. But from eight to eight-thirty where had Mark Denman been? He could easily have been in the stacks. According to Miss MacIntyre, Dr. Tyndale had been taking a walk. Emil Schlachtman had been near the library at eight-thirty. And about President Mittoff's activities I had not inquired.

Benjamin Morris, Agnes Hubbard, Miss MacIntyre and Bertha Chase (or rather Mrs. Denman) had all admitted their presence in the library. But by their very admissions they had intended, and had so far succeeded, in freeing themselves of any complicity in the crime. Now, however, I began to doubt all their statements. When I reviewed them in the cramped darkness inside the counter, they all seemed a bit thin. Had a slight noise so easily deterred Agnes Hubbard from her resolution to hunt in the stacks for Benjamin Morris? Had Bertha Chase known no more of the crime than she had divulged in her delirium? Were Miss MacIntyre's fears for Dr. Tyndale as vague as she would have me believe, or did she know more than she was telling? And finally, had Benjamin Morris been as drunk as he

would have me believe? He had been acute enough
to remember a woman with cane, a cane which we
later discovered had had a rubber tip. It had left
marks on the glass floor. But later Benjamin Morris
had recalled the tapping sound made by the cane.
My thoughts were troubled by some fugitive remembrance. Then I had it. Miss MacIntyre's cane had
no rubber tip. I had heard it distinctly this very
afternoon, tapping on the cement walk as we had
strolled to the library. The boy had been right.
Cold beads of sweat broke out on my forehead. Then
some one else with a stick had been in the library that
Thursday evening, some one with a stick heavy
enough perhaps to deliver a blow at the base of
Don Crawford's brain. I tried to recall all the canes
I knew. But I could remember no others. Only Miss
MacIntyre used one, and that only occasionally.
But was it always the same stick? A picture of the
umbrella stand in the corner of her hallway flashed
to my mind. I could see two canes in it. Then I had
proved nothing after all. She had simply carried
the other stick. Benjamin Morris' second thought
had been wrong.

The silence in the library was oppressive. And
my thoughts were going around in circles. I caught
at vague fragments of ideas. The two dogs, the Phi
Beta Kappa keys, two canes, Bertha Chase rushing
into the library calling to Mark Denman. If only
the nurses had managed to detain her at the infirmary. Dr. Whitaker had telephoned me as soon
as they had discovered her absence. Why, in the

name of Heaven, did she have to disappear at the exact time when I had to rush off to the library? I recalled my sensations as I sat at the hall telephone talking to the doctor. And then from some dark corner of memory my subconscious mind presented to me an unrealized impression. As I had talked to Dr. Whitaker that afternoon, my eyes had roamed over the spacious hallway. I had seen the beautiful cherry lyre table, the heavy gilt mirror, the four straight-backed chairs, and the umbrella stand. And the umbrella stand had been empty! Miss MacIntyre had had one stick beside her on the porch. Strange that she had felt the need of it that afternoon when she so seldom carried it save to poke around in the garden.

I felt a flash of inspiration that almost blinded me. My head reeled. I wondered if I were about to faint. For in that instant I had realized with singular clarity who had been threatening Dr. Tyndale. And I knew as surely as if the name had been spoken close to my ear who it was who had murdered Don Crawford. Everything fell into place, the two devoted dogs, Oscar Bartlett's Phi Beta Kappa key, the blow inflicted on Bertha Chase, the two figures who had rushed past me in the rotunda and sent me sprawling, the attack on Benjamin Morris as he bent to examine the marks of the cane, the disappearance of the two gold links — all the mysteries that had disturbed me were clarified. I knew the reasons for all that had occurred, the despairing hopes that had involved first one person then another in the sequence of tragedies. Only the primary cause remained shadowy, and that, I knew, involved past events of which I was ignorant. Only one person could tell of them, the one person for whom I now waited with both expectation and dread.

To prove to myself in yet another way that my surmise was a conviction, I reviewed the attitudes of all the persons, including Emil Schlachtman, at the moment when I had invited them to the afternoon gathering in the rotunda. They had all behaved naturally — too naturally. One person among them had overplayed his part. And so, by a second method, I checked my first conclusion.

Darkness had now filled the library, and with the evening coolness the building began to creak and whisper. What horrors was Poe relating to Wilkie Collins back there in the stacks? And Lady Macbeth — was she reliving ancient hopes or looking despairingly at that little drop of blood on her palm? I felt the terror of all recorded crime breathing around me. And I could only crouch, stiff and uncomfortable in my cave, waiting for a pair of footsteps to put the period to the past four days of mystery.

My legs were numb; I was hungry and thirsty; but tired as I was, sleep did not tempt me. I was spared that one agony as I waited, tense and nervous.

Time drifted past me, a lost denominator, until at the great front door I heard a tremendous rattle of keys. The door was flung open, and the yellow light of a flash circled the rotunda. Silently I shut myself into the counter. This would not be the person I awaited. This would be Emil Schlachtman on his eight o'clock rounds. He would punch the time clock inside the door and continue his rounds. Now, at least I knew the time, and I fancied that my vigil would continue until ten o'clock at the earliest. Then the main switch in the power house would remove all possibility of lights in the library. In the shadows of the rotunda the intruder could work unobserved.

But I could not risk detection by leaving my hiding place. So I waited, my muscles stiff, my heart beating thunderously in the small enclosed space. As time passed, the building set up all varieties of sound, a dull boom, a thin squeak, a hollow echo. Then suddenly my ears caught a new noise — a tiny scraping, close at hand. I scarcely breathed. No longer was I alone in the building.

Carefully I slid the door of my compartment to allow only a slit through which I could peer. I saw the quick furtive flash of a light upward, as brief as the flicker of a firefly. But evidently it had sufficed to locate the booklet. Then unmistakably I heard the sound of a chair lifted onto the table and some one mounting this height. The light flashed again and I saw a hand claw up toward the chandelier. But it fell a full three or four feet short of its purpose. Then with infinite precaution the figure descended. From my hiding place I could watch it, a darker shadow among the other shadows of the rotunda. It was not my purpose to let it escape. But I should not intrude until the booklet was actually in the hand of the shadow.

There came a sound now of something thrown upward. It fell to the floor, not loudly, but with a sibilant slither that told me a rope was being employed. Again it was tossed upward. This time it did not fall back. It had caught on the heavy grille work. And now the plan was evident. The shadow climbed again onto the table. I heard the sound of harsh breathing, as, hand over hand, it shortened the distance to the chandelier. I pushed open the door of the counter. I gathered myself together for a rush into the rotunda. And at that moment, with the detonation of an exploding bomb, the great chandelier gave way. It crashed to the floor, burying beneath it the shadowy weight that had caused its collapse. As I rushed into the rotunda I heard groans, agonized and stifled. I had no light to direct me, but I called his name.

"Dr. Tyndale," I shouted. "Dr. Tyndale, are you badly hurt?"

CHAPTER XXII

A SHRIEK, terrifying in its intensity, filled the rotunda and echoed with hideous overtones in the great dome. I ran toward the fallen heap of ironwork and attempted to lift it from the man pinned beneath the heavy weight. After that one horrible scream he had been silent, but now, as I attempted to relieve him, his groans sounded, low and hopeless.

"Can you move at all?" I asked.

"Only one leg," he answered in a muffled, tired voice.

With all my strength, I tugged at the large chandelier, but I could only shift the weight a bit, and, working in the dark as I was, I feared to inflict further injury on the man.

Suddenly, beside me, I heard another voice. "Tom, oh, Tom, you're all right, aren't you?" It was Carla, appearing like an angel at the right moment. How she had happened to come I could not inquire yet. First we must relieve the old man lying there on the floor. His moans were pitiful to hear, but I steeled

237

myself, remembering that he had killed Don Crawford. He might, however, be badly injured and
there was much that he must tell me.

"Carla, have you a light?" I asked.

She produced one immediately. "I was afraid
to use it," she said. "I thought perhaps it was you
who had screamed."

As she flashed the light downward we saw the
stricken face of the old scholar. Carla caught at my
arm. "Tom, it can't be real," she cried. "It can't
be Dr. Tyndale. I don't understand."

I made no attempt to explain.

"Push a chair over here," I directed, keeping my
hold on the chandelier. "Do you think you could
help me prop this up on the chair?"

Together we tugged and lifted until we had raised
one corner of the chandelier onto the chair. Dr. Tyndale gave a long sigh. "Can you move now?" I
asked him.

He lay quiet on the floor, relieved of the weight,
but only one arm responded to his effort. It was
evident that the old man was badly hurt.

"Carla, will you telephone Dr. Whitaker? Ask
him to get an ambulance and drive up to the front
entrance of the library. Tell him to hurry and not to
mind the grass." I handed her the flashlight. "And,
Carla, be sure to tell him this is the last accident
we'll have."

I heard her draw a sharp breath as she walked
toward the semicircular desk where the telephone
is located.

I knelt beside Dr. Tyndale. "We'll have you out of here in a little while," I said.

"Well, Allen, you caught me at last, didn't you?" he replied. "Though Denman nearly got ahead of you several times." His breath was labored and he spoke in uneven jerks.

"But Denman's methods were too crude. You used your head." He was silent a moment. "I believe I'm done for, Allen. And I'd like you to know that I didn't intend to kill Crawford. We'd ordered a batch of books together, and he'd taken that booklet of Lamb's as part of his share. When I discovered the value of it I was beside myself. I was desperate for money, but he wouldn't promise to divide."

"I think he intended to," I interrupted. I recalled Don's statement about there being a rather nice ethical point involved.

"Well, he didn't tell me about it if he did," Dr. Tyndale continued. "Once three years ago when we'd clubbed together in a purchase, a good book fell to my lot. Not so valuable as this, worth only two hundred dollars, but I wouldn't split. He was quite angry." (Ah, yes, I thought, that explained Don's' departure from Miss MacIntyre's house.) "We hadn't ordered any books together until last month. Strange, isn't it?" His old voice quavered. "I don't blame him, you know. And I'm sorry I killed him. But I was desperate." The old man's stertorous breathing alarmed me.

Carla slipped to my side. "It's all right. They'll

be here in a few minutes," she said. "Oh, Tom, isn't it awful that it's Dr. Tyndale?" She seemed to have forgotten that he was conscious, but he had heard her.

"It's not Dr. Tyndale," he said. "It's Oscar Bartlett. Mr. Denman was right. I'm not a doctor. Just a professor."

He was breathing feebly now. Then he began to whisper. "Let me talk," he said. "Let me tell all I can. I feel very strange. I must talk while I can. Then — "

Carla ran for a glass of water. It revived him momentarily. "Blackmail," he said weakly. "Blackmail for three years. Emil Schlachtman. Knew me in Heidelberg. Janitor there. Knew I'd plagiarized my dissertation. Everybody knew. Disgrace. My cousin and I were doing graduate work there. But I didn't kill James Tyndale." His voice was strong now and loud. Carla clutched my arm. "I didn't kill my cousin. He was brilliant, good. Stuck to me through disgrace. But he drowned. I tried to save him. He was my only relative — both of us orphans — looked alike. I came home to this country. Couldn't find work. Then five years later I took my cousin's name. I pretended I was James Tyndale. A wonderful idea. I came here to teach thirty years ago. And I was safe for twenty-seven years. Till Emil Schlachtmann came. He recognized me. Blackmail ever since. But not so much. A hundred now and then. Never five thousand before!"

He was silent. In the yellow light of the flash,

Carla and I looked down at his motionless body with its closed eyes.

"Poor man!" she said. But I hardened my heart. "Poor Don!" I exclaimed bitterly.

The old man opened his eyes. "I'm sorry," he said slowly. "I didn't mean to kill him. I was angry. I had a cane, and I brought it down on his neck before I thought. Then I went for water, and when that didn't revive him I pulled him over where you found him. I forgot to make a sliding mark though. Did you do that, Allen?"

"Yes," I said angrily, "I did that."

He chuckled faintly. "Ah, well, it doesn't matter now. It's all over."

There was a noise on the front steps. Carla ran to open the door. "It's Dr. Tyndale," I heard her say. "I believe he's dying."

Then Dr. Whitaker and two helpers were beside me. Carefully we lifted the old man onto the stretcher. He was unconscious now.

Dr. Whitaker's face was white and strained. "Allen," he said in a low voice, "are you sure this is the last?"

"Positive, sir," I replied. "I'll explain later."

The two attendants looked curiously at the broken chandelier.

"A tragic accident," I said. "But we can't go into that now."

Carefully we bore our burden out of the library and down the steps. Carla darted back into the building. Then she was beside me. "I'm going home, Tom," she said. "I have the booklet — and the rope, too."

"You're wonderful," I told her. "You think of everything. But are you all right? Will you be safe?"

"Perfectly, darling," she answered, and I climbed into the ambulance beside Dr. Whitaker and the recumbent figure.

The old man roused only once on the way to the infirmary. "Spare Miss MacIntyre," he whispered.

"We will," I promised.

When we carried him into the hospital he was dead.

"A broken neck," pronounced Dr. Whitaker a half hour later, "in addition to many other broken bones and probably internal injuries. It's a wonder he lived at all."

"It's a blessing he did," I answered, and I told him of the old scholar's confession and of my presence in the library.

"But good heavens, man, what a shock it must have been to you to discover it was Dr. Tyndale."

"No, not a shock," I answered. "You see, I'd just figured out it would be he who would return to the library."

"You mean you knew he was the murderer?"

"I thought so," I replied. "You see, there were too many clues. And I got to wondering why that was. Then all the significant clues began to disappear in the last two days — the two gold links and the rubber-tipped cane. I'm convinced now that was the lethal weapon. I believe that's the correct terminology. Well, it all pointed to one thing — some one who had been forgetful and absent-minded. And I remembered how absent-minded Dr. Tyndale was. Why, just this morning when I told him I was having a meeting in the library at four o'clock, he said, 'At four-thirty, you say?' So I began to expect him to-night."

But I had gone too fast for Dr. Whitaker. I had forgotten that there was a great deal he didn't know. So as we wandered toward President Mittoff's house, I gave him a brief resumé of my activities.

"The gold links near the body I could not identify," I said in conclusion. "And when they disappeared I suspected the two persons who had been in my room that day — Benjamin Morris and President Mittoff — though I would just as soon you kept that latter suspicion under your hat. Then later I remembered the Phi Beta Kappa key on Napoleon's collar and the gold chain which had fastened it there. I wondered if the links had been part of that chain. And I recalled that Dr. Tyndale might have slipped into my room that afternoon.

"Then I began to think of the companionship of those two dogs. I had always felt obscurely bothered by that. And all at once it began to seem symbolic. I wondered if there were not a bond between their owners. And then, far-fetched as my notion was, things began to click. It seemed strange that the initials of Oscar Bartlett formed the name of Emil

Schlachtman's dog. I wondered if there were some purpose there. I began to realize that Emil himself might have found the key and chain on the floor of the stacks. His dog had a way of wandering about in the library, accompanied, of course, by Dr. Tyndale's Scotty. And if Dr. Tyndale had absent-mindedly been wearing his own Phi Beta Kappa key with the name Oscar Bartlett on it and had wrenched it off there by Don's body on Thursday evening, what more cruel way could Emil have found to acquaint Dr. Tyndale with his discovery than by fastening it to Napoleon's collar and sending the little dog home. Behind it all I began to glimpse a motive of blackmail, though how Dr. Tyndale could have fallen into the power of such a man as Emil Schlachtman baffled me until Dr. Tyndale, with his dying breath, confessed. As I look back on it now, I realize that it was the refinement of cruelty that Emil should have named his dog Obie — a constant reminder to Dr. Tyndale that his secret was safe only so long as he continued to meet Emil's demands. For, of course, academic prestige meant more to the old man than anything in the world."

Dr. Whitaker was astounded. "Allen," he said, "you've missed your calling. You should be with Pinkerton."

I felt gratified, but not convinced. I had blundered many times, I knew, but in my narration I had not stressed these errors.

But my real satisfaction came in acquainting President Mittoff with the outcome. We found him at work in his study, and as I told my story I watched his face closely. Amazement, horror, incredulity, pity were recorded there.

"I must have a written report of this, Allen," he said as I concluded. "Only then shall I be able to grasp it. I have misjudged you, young man. I have not given you credit for your powers. But I shall make restitution. You shall not go unrewarded. And, by the way, will you conduct me to Emil Schlachtman's domain at nine in the morning?"

I agreed, and Dr. Whitaker and I took our departure. "He meant a raise," said Dr. Whitaker slyly as we went down the walk. "A raise is a fine thing for a married man."

I thought of that remark on my way home. And so, late as the hour was, I could not forbear walking past Carla's house. There was a light in her room. I know the way of pebbles against a screen. Soon she was on the porch beside me.

"I just remembered that you called me 'darling' to-night," I said. "What did you mean by that?"

"Darling," she replied.

And after an interval I recalled that I was hungry in another way, too. "I'm starving," I said. "Will you go up to George and Harry's with me? I think they're open all night."

"I'm hungry, too," she confessed. "I was in that old library from six o'clock on."

"You were! Carla, what were you doing there?"

"Hiding in the stacks waiting to protect you," she laughed.

"But how did you know I was there?"

"I just guessed. I thought there wasn't much in that story you told Miss MacIntyre."

I was thankful that the others had not been so distrustful of my statements as this girl who had just agreed to entrust her life to me.

"Weren't you scared?" I asked.

"Petrified," she said coolly. "Especially when I saw a figure crawl in the window."

"So old Dr. Tyndale knew about the windows, too," I mused as we gulped down sandwiches and coffee. "I'm really a rotten detective," I confessed. "I should have guessed it was Dr. Tyndale from the first. He must have been the person I saw in the stacks Friday evening. He had probably just recalled that Don Crawford had been writing in a book when he struck at him. I imagine the old man replaced the book on its shelf Thursday evening, and then later wondered about the notation. I couldn't have been the only one who saw him hunting there Friday night. Mark Denman saw him too. That's why the whole section of books was moved into his office. And that's how he found out the value of the Lamb booklet. A pity Don wasn't more explicit. If he'd only written 'Tyndale' instead of 'the knave.'

"Of course it was Dr. Tyndale who struck down Bertha Chase." (I could not yet call these people by their rightful names.) "And to think he had the booklet in his hands for a few moments then. He must have dropped it when Mark Denman chased him. If Dr. Tyndale had sold it, he might never have been discovered. I suppose Emil told him this was his last demand. I rather think he planned to go back to Heidelberg. He mentioned something about it to me."

"But, Tom, who followed us that night we took the booklet from the office? Was it Mark Denman?"

"I think not," I replied. "I'd been followed earlier that evening. I think it was Dr. Tyndale. He knew I'd got wind of something, and he was counting on my leading him to the booklet. I almost did, too," I reflected. "He must have used the beech tree to get in and out of the house without observation. The branches extended under his window, too. He was on to all my tricks. It's you, Carla, who really solved the mystery by finding out where Denman had hidden the booklet."

"That was nothing," she said. "I just wanted to prove to you I could help."

I shuddered as I thought to what dangers she had exposed herself. What if Dr. Tyndale had caught up with us? He had been desperate to the point of madness by then.

"Why do you suppose Dr. Tyndale didn't kill Emil Schlachtman and have done with it? Poor Don, there was no reason for him to die."

"I don't suppose it ever occurred to him," I said. "He didn't really mean to kill Don. He just hit him in a fit of anger. He'd probably borrowed the cane when he went for his walk and then stopped in the library for some reason. The rest just happened."

"And Benjamin Morris — who hit him?"

"The same person, I imagine, and with the same stick. Perhaps Benjamin's actions seemed suspicious. He was down on his hands and knees, you know, looking at the marks Dr. Tyndale's stick had left. You know, Carla, it's strange the affair took so long to solve when it was really so obvious. Bertha Chase and Miss MacIntyre both saw Don unconscious by the table. I suppose that was when Dr. Tyndale was off getting water to revive Don. He must have skulked around a lot avoiding people, but I don't suppose he ever guessed any one had seen Don at the table. Otherwise he would never have moved the body, even to make it look accidental. My notion is that Miss MacIntyre found the cane there by the table, and recognizing it as her own, simply carried it home. Maybe she suspected Dr. Tyndale all the time. She accompanied him there the first thing in the morning, probably intending to protect him. She knew how absent-minded he was."

"Oh, how could she?" Carla cried.

"Easily," I answered. "I can understand it. She was very fond of him. And she knew he was in trouble of some sort. Emil Schlachtman used that poor wife of his to threaten Dr. Tyndale. Miss MacIntyre even saw her from a distance, but of course she didn't know who it was. And now that rubber-tipped cane has disappeared. Miss MacIntyre must have hidden it. I wonder how much of it all she suspected."

"Yes," Carla smiled a little wanly. "I suppose she

would shield him. You even suspected me for a while, didn't you?"

"Forgive me." I took her hand across the table of the deserted restaurant. "I never stopped loving you."

"I know. I had one awful hour myself."

We walked home slowly through the deserted streets, and I thought what changes had occurred in four days, what sorrow, anxiety, fear and joy. It was just as well that I did not know that the coming day was to hold further anxiety and grief: that President Mittoff and I were to discover that Emil Schlachtman had fled before we arrived, leaving his wife to corroborate helplessly Dr. Tyndale's revelation of blackmail; and that when I told her of Dr. Tyndale's accidental death, Miss MacIntyre was to sink gently into a faint from which she never regained consciousness. No, I did not think of the morrow nor of the day to come when I should find Miss MacIntyre's rubber-tipped cane buried in the garden where she must have hidden it that Sunday night when she had muddied her white shoes. I did not think of the dismissal of the Denmans and of their matrimonial woes, or of the hopes of Agnes Hubbard and Benjamin Morris. If I thought of the future at all, it was to see in it a picture of Carla and me wandering happily through these village streets and not parting, as we were doing now, at the door of Mrs. Titcomb's house.

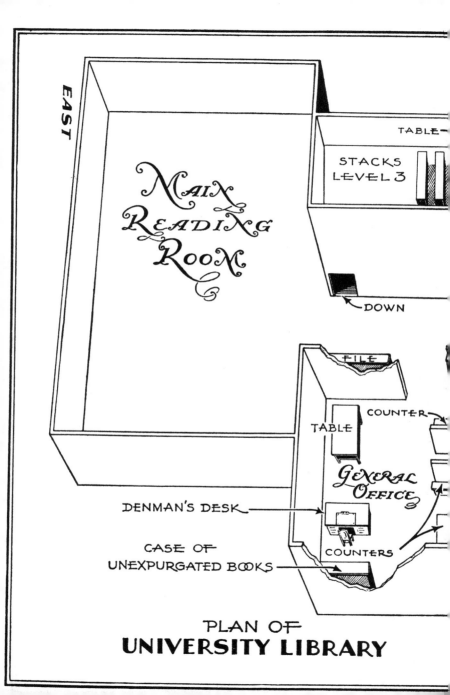

EAST

$\mathcal{M}$ain $\mathcal{R}$eading $\mathcal{R}$oom

STACKS LEVEL 3

TABLE—

←DOWN

FILE

COUNTER—

TABLE

$\mathcal{G}$eneral $\mathcal{O}$ffice

DENMAN'S DESK——

CASE OF UNEXPURGATED BOOKS——

COUNTERS

PLAN OF
UNIVERSITY LIBRARY